God Bless America

By Harri Rob

God Bless America

For information address:
info@mickiedaltonfoundation.com

First Published in 2014 in Australia

ISBN: 978-0-9923422-8-9

Published by The Mickie Dalton Foundation
NSW
Australia
www.mickiedaltonfoundation.com

Chapter 1

The incredible prejudice taking place towards the AIDS sufferer is almost common practice in the major hospitals throughout America with the stigma towards the AIDS patient now spreading to all parts of the globe.

Linda, a reporter with the Weekly Courier hoped to change a few things by completing a series of articles directed towards bringing the need for compassion about the sufferer to the notice of the American public. True, a story done and re-done, but she was totally convinced within herself that not enough forgiveness or caring had been directed into the articles written earlier. She had discreetly spent months of her own time at the San Francisco Greater Library researching the AIDS virus and its early development into the killer of mankind.

The doctors and so-called experts of the late 70s and early 80s blamed the homosexual for the creation of the virus. However, the truth be known and it's still out there, there is not a scrap of evidence to support their theories.

Since 1974 when the HIV virus was first isolated, nineteen million people have perished throughout the world. And the sad truth is that a further thirty-five million were diagnosed with the virus by 2012. All are waiting to die a death so lonely and painful only the sufferer could fully understand the isolation awarded them in their final moments of life.

The infection rates throughout the world, be it by ignorance, needle sharing, unsafe sex, or as in Africa's case, children born with the virus, have now reached plague proportions. Every year the ratio of AIDS increases by 15%, meaning that this year, 2014, at least forty million will perish within the next ten years. The truth about AIDS has never been clarified and the people who are in the know are still keeping us in the dark for whatever reasons we can only guess. A leading researcher with a conscience had ominously sent unsigned letters to the Weekly. The letters contained the DNA breakdown of the deadly HIV virus and how he had stumbled upon and isolated a chromosome belonging only to man. The chromosome did not appear anywhere on the evolutionary tree relating to monkeys and he couldn't comprehend how a human chromosome had somehow entered the monkey version of HIV giving us the deadly formula we know today. Even by rapid mutation, the transformation of this chromosome is impossible. He also made it clear about the multinational drug companies and how they were holding the world to ransom by exploiting the expenses associated with the medicines and vaccines used to prolong life, but not to cure.

The anonymous researcher through his letters hoped the Courier would follow up his findings and not bury the truth, thus informing an unsuspecting world that the AIDS virus now ravaging the planet had not originated from the homosexual sector or mutated from apes of Africa as we are led to believe.

Linda's only available research into the virus brought her to the baboons of Central Africa, blaming the locals for creating this new virus by their homosexual acts towards the male monkeys. These articles had been published in

1978 by the American Disease Control Centre and though they contained certain dates to the early outbreak of the virus, collectively they made no sense. The Centre had for years been blaming the homosexual for the outbreak and the spreading of the virus throughout the world. Their articles are like slinging mud; if enough is thrown, some will stick.

The people who controlled the centre in the early seventies were FBI personnel under the control of J. Edgar Hoover. But sadly as the personnel changed over the years, their beliefs didn't. Though this was not really what Linda wanted to write about, it was her only source of research. To her dislike there were too many twists and turns and too many learned scientists unwilling to divulge findings which could collectively help solve the mystery of how AIDS had virtually created itself.

Deep down she really didn't want to believe the assorted details that she was now discovering, but one thing was for sure. The files she'd extracted from the San Francisco library continually contradicted themselves. If you were to believe American research gathered by J Edgar Hoover's people in the seventies and released to the public by the American Disease Control Centre, then AIDS definitely came out of central Africa by the sodomy and sexual acts carried out by the locals towards the resident baboons.

But if you followed the English theories, the virus was conceived by homosexuals and their need to constantly swap partners. Both beliefs became widely accepted. But the argument still rages about the virus's beginnings.

The first known case of AIDS occurred in New York, June 16th, 1974 in the homosexual sector then two weeks later in San Francisco, another reported case was discovered amongst the homosexuals.

The evidence supporting the English theory seemed overwhelming at the time, as only homosexuals of that era were affected. Linda wanted to release to her readers the last thoughts, wishes and regrets of the terminally ill, the humane side to the virus, the true feelings of the stricken before they departed life, not the illicit side on which so many earlier articles had focused. She didn't want to enter the debate as to where and when AIDS created itself.

The Courier, though only a small independent magazine and sometimes struggling for recognition amongst the giants of news-corps, paid its way by doing follow up stories that centred more on the humane issues, with a clearer definitive detailed background, not the impact reporting carried out by the large powerful tabloids of San Francisco. Linda spent weeks scouring the major hospitals, searching for that special patient with a story to tell, but everywhere she turned for help, doors closed before her. Doctors whom she had met socially and thought were friends became reluctant to discuss the issues surrounding the virus and thus her story started to become an obsession so entrenched in her mind that she would now move heaven and earth to achieve her goals and hopefully finally publish the truth, proving to the world that this was not a virus to be swept under the carpet.

It was a virus so deadly that an immediate finding is needed to stop or control the death toll now taking place on the planet. America so far has spent 120 billion dollars on getting rid of Saddam Hussein and but less than .001% on AIDS research! Can we really justify the few people elected to power by us to making these loose and devious decisions? She also hoped to form a foundation on the net that would allow the aids sufferers to share their thoughts and sorrows amongst themselves without being ridiculed and tormented for having the virus.

Chapter 2

On the morning of March 7 2013, standing silently alone in Ward Six of the San Francisco Central Hospital, Linda felt ill at the ever present lingering smell of heavy mildew seeping from the caverns of the walls. A frail, helpless figure lay before her, oblivious to life. She noticed the wall chart at the foot of the patient's bed. The graph, unusually low hovering towards the bottom and reflecting the number 73, the same number being on the patient's armband.

Only days earlier, the patient had been flung from a speeding vehicle onto the main steps of the hospital suffering from a horrific beating received in the privacy of his hotel room. The hospital's resident detective had found it impossible to discover an identity and tracing the patient's last movements had been almost impossible. When the hotel where he had last stayed was finally located, it was only because the night porter at the Allah Ritz had recognized his identity photo circulated throughout the hotels and motels of San Francisco. His record contained nothing relating to check-in time or financial transactions. His personal belongings had mysteriously vanished as though he hadn't existed. Someone didn't want this man identified and being an AIDS sufferer nobody really cared.

Chapter 3

Located high in the valleys overlooking the city. its rolling hills dotted by suburbia leading to the Golden Gate, San Francisco Medical Centre was the only research facility into AIDS operating in the immediate area. The entire west wing had been privately donated to the research of HIV, and was funded not by the state, but by the private sector.

Over the weeks that Linda had been visiting, her friendship with some nurses had flourished, making movement throughout the wards easier and less obtrusive. On the morning of March ninth, she stood silently at the foot of 73's bed, observing the frail facial movements of the patient. The eyes were in a state of REM (Rapid Eye Movement) when a nurse entered the ward and made her way towards her.

"Any change Linda?" she asked, her footsteps from her standard issue shoes, echoing quietly around the room.

"No," Linda replied, her spirits immediately lifting as she always enjoyed Karen's input. "Why are his eyes continually moving?" she asked.

"The patient is comatose, the eyes are the window to his soul, showing brain activity. And believe me, that's good."

"Has anyone requested a dental check?" asked Linda.

"Yes. Everything humanly possible has been tried to ID the patient, but there's one thing you need to understand. He's an AIDS sufferer and that don't open any doors. Not in this world." Karen smiled sadly.

"I see! Everyone passes the buck!" Linda said, observing the injustice of the frail figure laying in the bed, helpless and oblivious to any human presence.

"Absolutely, take a look at this," Karen said as she slid on a pair of surgical gloves and gently opened 73's mouth, trying carefully not to cause him further discomfort.

"You're kidding!" Linda gasped, not believing what her eyes were seeing. "What sick person would want to inflict that much pain? Oh my God, look at his teeth. What the fuck have these ass-holes done?" she continued, not believing what her eyes were telling her.

"I've no idea. But, I'm certain he was awake during the ordeal," Karen replied.

"How could you possibly know that?" Linda asked.

"Look at the bruising at the back of his neck, it definitely shows signs of resistance," Karen replied as she gently turned the patient's head, lifting it from the pillow.

"Couldn't these injuries have occurred when he was thrown from the speeding vehicle?"

"No, Linda! Not these injuries. Someone didn't want this man found. I'm convinced they thought he was dead long before he hit the pavement."

"Then how could you possibly know he was awake while these sadistic bastards mutilated his mouth?" A cold shiver spiralled up Linda's spine. The nerve ends throughout the patient's mouth were separately exposed. His teeth had been either violently ripped out or ferociously filed flat, making any dental search useless. His tongue in the process had been badly lacerated as had his gums.

"Isn't there something we can do to help this guy?" Linda asked.

"Not unless you find the people responsible and the reason why they're trying to eliminate him."

"What about the police?" Linda asked.

"They don't want anything to do with terminally ill AIDS patients," the nurse replied as she put the patient's head back on the pillow. "Linda, it's a fact of life. These people are classed already dead, because no-one cares."

"Somebody has to," Linda said, moved by her feelings of mingled anger and horror. "Wouldn't DNA give us an answer? Or at least a clue as to who he is."

"He has no DNA comparison. No known records. Any test would be futile," the nurse said. "Linda, honestly, there's no-one. But with your persistence and patience, perhaps you can succeed where everyone else failed." A smile reappeared on her face as she quietly departed the ward, her carefully trodden footsteps disappearing silently into the distance and a deafening silence returning to haunt the inner sanctums of the ward.

There were six beds in all spread around the ward, but only this bed, directly beneath the window was occupied. *With patients on trolleys lining the halls, why were the five spare beds not in use?* thought Linda. The whole scenario made no sense and each time she had made inquiries she received vague answers. Contamination was the hospital's main excuse. But with all her research into the virus and knowing it to be body fluid related, their answers were lies and didn't make sense. Linda had for days felt an uncomfortable undercurrent in her emotions every time she entered the hospital, especially Ward Six.

Karen, her only friendly nurse had now all but confirmed her uncertain feelings.

Chapter 4

Alone again, Linda quietly pondered the situation, but was not entirely happy with the two hours assigned her daily to observe 73. She desperately needed more time alone with the patient if any progress was to be made. Nor did she need the constant interruptions caused by some of the staff or the prying eyes each time she stood over and talked to the near-lifeless patient in the hope somehow of reaching his subconscious.

Linda moved discreetly to the main office located near the centre of the hospital and shaped as a large enclosed fish bowl, keeping her segregated from the inner space by a thick glass partition. She spoke to the secretary who was seated at a small desk partially covered by old newspapers. But the secretary completely ignored Linda's presence.

"Could I please speak to someone in charge?" Linda repeated with her voice now almost apologetic, her hands showing signs of a slight tremble, with the sweat on her palms uncomfortably cold with anticipation as she glared at this person sitting directly in front of her. Glancing around the office Linda couldn't help but notice the stick figures in the collective pictures hanging on the feature wall behind the secretary, reminding her of the scribbles drawn by the late John Lennon, but the name signed at the bottom was that of Adolph Hitler.

"The Superintendent has someone with him," the secretary said rudely, peering over the top of her dark-rimmed glasses. Her arms and neck were enormous and her double chin quivered long after she had finished speaking.

"It's important," Linda insisted, noticing the annoyance growing on the face of this huge woman with each passing moment.

"Are the pictures on the wall originals?" said Linda, hoping valiantly to win over the confidence of this massive woman who had now turned to face her.

"No, they're copies," the woman snapped. "But they're good, aren't they?" she added in a tone somewhat softer and expressing a desire to take the conversation further.

"Yes! I would not in a moment have picked them as copies," Linda answered politely.

"I'll see if Mr. Rineheart has the time to see you," the woman declared, but her body language made Linda aware that this could be a real problem. At least she felt comfortable that she had made the effort to ask the question, although the secretary looked more like a bouncer than a secretary nurse. As the huge figure moved towards the door of the inner office Linda caught a glimpse of what looked surprisingly like a swastika tattoo on the shirt line of her uniform across the bulk muscle of her left arm.

"Thanks," replied Linda, her mouth suddenly dry, trying to remain casual throughout the irritating moment. She could see what she thought was the head honcho and a woman arguing, with the occasional glance through the heavy glass partition checking her out, but she couldn't comprehend a problem. For every known reason, Linda felt she wasn't welcome and started to develop a deep perturbed feeling, but shook that off as paranoia.

Linda's eyes scoured the corridors, looking for a friendly face. Even Stan Mulligan, her worst nightmare at school, would have served the purpose, but sadly there were no friendly faces in sight. She seemed to wait an eternity with the arguing inside the inner office becoming incessant. A person on whom she had never laid eyes upon, an older woman dressed in red, looking ready to kill was arguing and waving her arms feverishly, seemingly in control, taking centre stage of the inner office, with the voices becoming ever louder. Suddenly standing before her, a large man approaching middle age, worry lines etched deep into his face, was looking through her, not at her.

"You wished to speak to me?" he asked abruptly. The sweat was thick on his brow, his voice cold and unconcerned and he was wearing a grey wrinkled suit that looked as though he'd slept in it.

"Thank you for seeing me on such short notice," replied Linda politely. But the fat man didn't answer nor did he acknowledge Linda's outstretched hand presented in a friendly gesture.

"I would like to monitor the patient in Ward Six," she went on. "And if possible, come to an arrangement with the hospital about doing a series of articles about terminally ill AIDS patients."

"You would, would you?" he answered. "I'm afraid we don't allow the press access to terminally ill patients, at least not without their consent."

"But I'm not the press!"

"I was told you are from the Weekly Courier! Or have I been misinformed?" the fat man asked with a half smile.

"No sir!" Linda answered. "The Courier is a weekly magazine owned by my dad. The stories we run relate more the human factor. Not the gossip reporting of the daily papers. We do in-depth stuff on the background of our subjects, and try to relate the feelings and compassion of our subjects to an insensitive public."

Linda's eyes kept returning to a blood stain that should have been removed eons ago, but had been left to linger beneath the layers of wax laid over the years to the highly polished old wooden floor.

"I see," replied the fat man, peering over his shoulder, waiting for confirmation from the inner office. "We don't want the public getting the wrong idea about our hospital and the research we do here! Do we?"

A cold stare had crept into his eyes, making Linda feel exceedingly uncomfortable.

"I'm aware of the rules about only immediate family allowed visiting critically ill patients but this is no ordinary person. For Christ sake, he's dying from AIDS. Let me at least do a sympathetic story on the man. It may even help pay for his funeral, when the time comes."

"Money is not an issue here. We are predominantly a research centre and we don't need publicity," he replied smiling sarcastically. "We are self funded and only responsible to the American Disease Control Centre which overlooks and controls all our findings."

"Sir you misunderstood me!" replied Linda. "I'm writing the sad truth about the people who have somehow contracted AIDS. Not an article about the hospital."

He stood staring directly at Linda for what seemed an eternity, then after a few brisk hand movements from the old woman in red, he finally replied.

"You are a persuasive young lady. I have been directed by my superior to relax some rules," he said as the mysterious woman again issued instructions with the movement of her hands. He paused, and then continued. "I'll make arrangements for you to be allowed to observe the patient between eight in the morning, after his bed bath, up-till five in the evening, before his needle program, but beyond that time you do not go. Understood?" His voice rose as he spoke, nearly shouting by the end.

"Needle program?" asked Linda. "I didn't think they injected HIV patients for fear of infection and the collapsing of the arteries!"

"Normally we don't. But he's a special case and the pills are clearly not working. Purely experimental," the man said hurriedly, again looking to the inner office for guidance but this time, none came. Linda didn't give the hollow words a second thought, she was more grateful for the chance afforded her to observe the patient undisturbed.

"Thank you! I'm sure you won't regret your decision," she said politely, finally shaking the man's hand, but that experience was like holding a wet fish.

"I already do," he sighed loudly.

This grossly overbearing person in a managerial position was becoming extremely annoying to Linda.

"I don't know what the problem is with this patient, but be assured, this will be good PR for the hospital and staff," she said concealing her frustrations.

"Again we're not that type of hospital. PR is not an issue. And as you put it, we don't have a problem with this patient. But, rules are rules and they most stringently will be obeyed. I really hope a mistake hasn't been made," said the domineering, unctuous man as he quickly disappeared back to the inner office, slamming the heavy glass door behind him, the stick pictures falling heavily to the floor, scattering glass to all corners of the corridor.

Linda felt she'd won a war, until now unattainable. How could this fat presumptuous public servant treat anyone so haughtily?

Chapter 5

Mick had been a close friend of Linda's for the past fifteen years. In fact, it was exactly twelve years to the day that they had both graduated from the San Francisco College of Journalism. Mick had been out of work on purpose for a couple of months but was unquestionably the most talented computer hacker in San Francisco. If Mick weren't surfing the net, he would be lost deep inside huge corporate computers, strictly for kicks, delving into their darkest secrets. He often thought of himself as a communal watchdog, many a time stumbling on corporate atrocities carried out by mindless, unrepentant multinational corporations. Quietly and anonymously, he would leak the story, complete in every detail to major papers, knowing full well that they would take the story further.

So damaging to some corporations had been some of Mick's hacking, that a reward of $1,000,000 was posted on the Internet for any information leading to the Happy Hacker, payable instantly. He had even thought about collecting his own reward, but stopped short of becoming brash. Mick had either designed the systems or software to infiltrate most any closed circuit network, including the levels locked away for the years to come. Information stored away under the National Securities Act, supposedly to protect the innocent but in most cases, was serving only to hide the guilty. The perfect example of the Secrecy Act in

America was the cover-up in the assassination of John Fitzgerald Kennedy. Not Lee Harvey Oswald or the Russians, as the FBI wanted the world to believe, but the late J. Edgar Hoover with the aid of the Mafia, had been responsible for the shooting from the infamous knoll. The whole assorted exercise had been financed by Fidel Castro. In fact, Lee Harvey Oswald was himself FBI, but sacrificed by the Bureau to cover any loose ends and embarrassing questions that may have arisen.

Mick had all the information available, but when he started downloading to his computer, the levels tapped into were being hurriedly erased. Information stored for forty-odd years, information for future generations gone forever. He understood perfectly that his adversaries monitoring his hacking were extremely dangerous and powerful.

Mick blamed both organizations, the FBI and CIA for the shredding of documents, but sadly couldn't prove his beliefs. But he also believed that one day, somehow, he would come across the evidence to validate his findings, allowing him to finally release to the American public and the world his beliefs about the two organizations. He only hoped it would be sooner rather than later, while the people responsible were still alive. Over the years, Mick had sometimes worked closely with the magazine, so his input to Linda's story could prove invaluable.

"Mick?" asked Linda. "How do you pay for all this time off you're constantly having? I mean, how do you cover the bills that never cease to come?"

"That's no secret. I simply sell new technology that I'm lucky enough to stumble upon from time to time."

"To whom?" she asked.

"There are people out there that will buy anything to do with software. They will buy it, they will manipulate it, and then claim they invented it!"

"Name one," said Linda.

"Gill Bates!" answered Mick immediately.

"Doesn't that bother you?" asked Linda.

"Not in the least. I'm getting well paid," replied Mick almost smiling.

"What about the recognition your ideas could bring to you!"

"Stuff the recognition. I don't need that crap. Is this conversation leading somewhere or are we merely chewing the fat?" He talked while pecking continually on the keyboard.

"Hopefully, you see, at the moment I'm working on bringing the compassionate side of AIDS to my readers. And I need your help."

"AIDS!" he exclaimed. "Sounds boring!" He leaned back in his chair, his hands behind his head and stretching.

"Maybe, but it's a story I feel I must write. These people are treated as second-class citizens and I don't like the injustice taking place." Linda took a seat by the desk. "Since 74 when the virus first hit the planet, nineteen million people have died from AIDS. And this year, a further forty-odd million infected with the virus will be waiting to die. In Africa alone, two hundred children are born daily carrying the virus. At today's rates these numbers will double every five years. Think about the famous that have already died. Liberace, Rock Hudson, Peter Allen, Freddie Mercury. The list goes on and on."

"Yes, but they chose their own path. They were raging homosexuals!" Mick looked up from the monitor and smirked.

"You don't have to be homosexual to contract AIDS."

"No but it helps!" replied Mick a sheepish smile crossing his lips, but not wanting to argue about something he felt he had no way of winning. "OK! I see your point. Where in hell did you get these figures?"

"It wasn't easy," replied Linda. "And sadly, the source is controlled by the American Disease Control Centre and for some obscure reason, they still seem intent on the theory that AIDS created itself. Also an anonymous researcher whom I'm sure dad knows has for the past three weeks has been sending findings to the Courier, findings that would curl the hairs on the back of your neck."

"What findings?" asked Mick.

"He claims that AIDS is a monkey virus carried commonly by baboons."

"And that little revelation is going to curl the hairs on the back of my neck?"

"No!" replied Linda sarcastically. "He states specifically that the monkey virus carried by the baboons of Haiti is exactly the same as the human virus!"

"Go on!" replied Mick, turning from the keyboard and giving Linda his undivided attention.

"Ok! Knowing that both viruses are exactly the same and he stresses that before 1974, there was no such recorded virus relating to mankind, how could a human chromosome present itself in this predominantly monkey orientated virus? How come in this modern age of technology no-one can explain successfully how or why that 23rd chromosome entered into the human virus?" She stirred restlessly in her seat. "We humans only have twenty-two chromosomes. The twenty third is not possible. It cannot cross over."

"Linda! Look at the mad cow disease and how that has crossed the human boundaries!" Mick said with a smile.

"Not even similar. The mad cow disease was created by the British scientists feeding the cattle back to themselves and then us eating them. Sure, if sanity prevails then it's only a matter of time before something goes wrong. But this is different. The said chromosome now comes into play. How did it get into a human virus?"

"Exactly what are you implying?" he asked, looking interested for the first time.

"I'm implying someone, somehow had to do some tampering. Anything is better than nothing. I don't know! And the frustration is that, that's where my research ends But truly what really matters are the numbers of people dying from the virus. Dying in ridicule and in silence and no one giving a shit about their pleas!"

"You really feel that compelled? And you honestly think that I can make a difference?" said Mick.

"I do! Please Mick will you help with the story?"

"Knowing you and your passion for a good read, and what you have already told me, how can any red blooded person say no?" replied Mick, a smile creeping into the corner of his mouth while nodding approval.

"This is something you will never regret," said Linda. "Hopefully we can somehow help these people. Hopefully we're going to right a wrong. Hopefully."

"What the hell. It's not like I've got something better to do!" said Mick sarcastically, with his eyes lifting to the ceiling.

"Thanks!" she replied pecking him gently on the cheek and extremely grateful for his help with her story.

"Linda! Who is this researcher sending all this unsolicited information? And how do you know he's genuine?"

"I don't! But he must have medical experience because of the way he states things. Some of the things in his letters seem to come directly from medical journals. Dad thinks he knows who he is but is at this stage reluctant to tell me his name."

"Could I see these letters?" asked Mick.

"Sure. I'll pick them up tomorrow from dad's office," she replied ending the conversation.

Chapter 6

Howard McAllister, Linda's father, editor, publisher and owner of the magazine made it clear he would do all he could to support the story. However, funds were extremely tight at the moment and there would be expenses at times that could simply not be justified. Linda would have to do most of her research on her own time and even pay some of the incurred expenses. Whatever was needed!

Linda, whose friend William, the most respected reporter at the magazine as well as the highest paid, agreed to help with the background research and the monitoring of this unusual patient. Linda had only recently returned from covering the expanding AIDS story of Africa where one third of Africans, mostly children now carry the virus. Most are born with AIDS and with no medicines or vaccines available to the mostly third world Nations of the continent.

It was only a matter of time before much of the continent crumbles into a human catastrophe. The major drug companies throughout the world won't release cheap drugs into Africa and the African governments, riddled by corruption and scandal won't address the issue of AIDS, saying that they don't have a problem with the virus.

Linda knew she had a massive task on her hands.

Chapter 7

Gathering all their available information, Linda along with Bill set up a small table at the foot of 73's bed. Here they could quietly research, using her laptop, this unforgiving plague while praying for a minor miracle, all the time closely watching 73 fighting for his life. Mick had installed a voice-activated recorder together with a motion-sensitive camera to help monitor 73's movements in the long lonely hours of the night. Any information they gathered could be analysed back at the apartment. But so far, nothing!

Days came and went with no sign of life. Their cause seemed futile, for the seemingly lifeless body lying before them was rapidly deteriorating and wasting away.

On the eighth morning, Linda noticed the intravenous drip attached to 73's arm had ceased to function. The clear sterile bag hanging from the hospital tree had been almost empty the previous afternoon, yet no one had bothered changing to a new plasma drip, again highlighting the plight of the conveniently forgotten.

Then on the tenth day, standing alone at the foot of 73's bed, Bill noticed a small ray of sunlight peeking through a tear in the old blind, the sunlight touching the corner of the patient's left eye. His weakened body was trying in vain to move away from the light. A frail discoloured hand covered in tiny festering white blisters lifted cautiously towards his face, blocking out the bright glow from the sun. Sensing a sign and needing to take full advantage of the situation, Bill moved quickly to reach 73's subconscious and it wasn't but a moment before the eyes, closed for so long, slowly opened.

Standing silently, Bill observed the expressions on the tortured face of the person in the bed before him. Both eyes with enormous cataracts, almost to the point of blindness, expressed a painfully evident fear as to the uncertainty of knowing whether amongst friends or enemies, who or where he was and possibly remembering the brutal beating he'd received weeks earlier.

He lay looking back at Bill, his eyes barely open, asking the questions but uttering no sound. Bill moved cautiously to introduce himself, hopeful of erasing the tension that seemed to stand between them, and to convince this patient that he was on his side and would move heaven and earth to help in any way possible.

"The name's Bill. Sorry, William, William Hackett," said Bill in an unusually soft tone as the patient's eyes stared glaringly deep into Bill's soul, searching for a reason to believe. "I'm a friend. I'm here to help" said Bill as 73's eyes squinted and looked suspiciously at the person standing at the end of his bed.

"If you can comprehend or understand a word I'm saying, please blink three times," said Bill, hoping that somehow he could reach 73's conscious mind.

The answers from his erratic movements came slowly as he shuffled beneath the sheets trying desperately to communicate, with only hollow gasps of breath breaking the silence. The walls aligning 73's bed had been hurriedly painted a sickly grey, to cover the creeping mould now well established in the ward. The paint on the ceiling constantly flaked to the floor and at times could be mistaken for snow, or a swarm of white butterflies exiting from their cocoons whenever a heavy vehicle passed by the hospital. The old wooden floor was also well past its use by date and urgently needed repair. Holes dotted sections of the ward allowing the weather to dominate conditions of the room as the air conditioning in this part of the hospital being a luxury reserved only for the staff, with only the plush offices cleaned regularly.

Realizing something was desperately wrong and communication beyond him, 73's eyes stared glaringly at Bill, and then slowly blinked.

"The hospital requested a dental search, but due to the state of your teeth," Bill continued carefully, "they found it impossible to establish a positive identification."

Slowly and cautiously, 73's withered fingers turned blue through the lack of circulation and covered in small white festering blisters felt his mouth, a tiny tear appearing in the corner of his eyes. No doubt the memories were flooding back as the pain on his face became alarmingly apparent.

"I asked the Federal Bureau of Investigation for a fingerprint match, but that too turned up negative," said Bill.

73's eyes widened as a profound fear became apparent on his face. Somehow, something was desperately wrong, so quickly and deliberately Bill changed the subject and as he did, Linda walked quietly through the door, looking the picture of elegance. Her short mini complimented the long shapely legs and the shine of her healthy strawberry blonde hair, accentuated the exuberance of youth.

Bill felt that there'd been something in what he'd said that upset 73, but he felt now wasn't the time to pursue the issue. The following hour was taken up telling 73 about themselves, their research and goals in trying to understand the twilight hours of persons suffering from the virus the feelings of their loved ones, possible regrets, the tiniest diminutive hopes, with any last wishes needed to be fulfilled before departing this life. Time had somehow quickly slipped away and was now well past the hour of five, their agreed cut-off point, so leave they must, but would eagerly return early tomorrow, hopefully come to an arrangement about publishing his story. Turning to walk away, a faint voice from behind cried out.

"Please don't abandon me!"

Bill instinctively turned to witness 73 up on one elbow, straining, begging them not to leave without him. Linda had earlier made intensive inquiries about moving the patient to more comfortable quarters, hopefully a private room gladly paid for by the Weekly. But mysteriously the answer received was a staunch no.

Advanced AIDS patients would not leave Ward Six alive. In his fatigued state, 73 signalled for Linda to move closer, his voice rapidly becoming too weak and feeble to recognize. Bending silently over his bed, she moved closer, straining to hear his tortured words. Bill in his frustration couldn't hear their conversation, but witnessed the pain evident on 73's face as he despairingly tried to communicate with Linda.

At the same moment, a nurse entered the ward, someone Bill had never laid eyes on and by her enormous size commanded respect. Moving quickly towards them, she thundered her warning, as the white paint from the ceiling flaked heavily to the floor and if it wasn't for the seriousness of her tone would have been almost comical. This huge figure, covered in white flakes pushing through a corridor of fluttering white butterflies of all shapes and sizes.

"It's past the hour of five. You must leave immediately! This patient is due to receive his injections," echoed loudly around the room, the flakes still tumbling softly to the old wooden floor.

Again the injections, thought Bill, carefully replying in his quietly spoken voice.

"Sorry, nurse! We'll only be a moment. We promise to use less of your precious time tomorrow!" His statement incensed her as she screamed back.

"Your hours are over. You were told till five. Hospital policy will be upheld!"

The tone of her voice was becoming deeper each passing moment.

Bill witnessed the annoyance on her face as 73 continued to whisper his hidden message to Linda. The huge figure of the nurse reminded Bill of a Gestapo sergeant he'd seen in a movie as a young boy, but never expected to meet.

"Are you German?" asked Bill in his satirical voice.

"I'll call security if you don't leave immediately," was the reply. Calling security was not an option, her size alone frightened Bill and as her voice turned cold, he became wary.

"It's time to leave, sweetie! Mustn't break the rules," said Bill sarcastically.

He gently took Linda by the arm, they turned to witness this huge figure in a completely uncontrolled outburst throw the needles and vaccine to the floor then storm out of the ward, the white paint again moving heavily from the ceiling long after her thunderous footsteps had departed.

"I hope I didn't cause her to lose her cool," he said smiling, but Linda didn't reply. She merely shook her head, as she suspected Bill's outburst hadn't helped their cause.

"Please take me," continued the repeated cries in a weak wavering tone, unable to complete the sentence.

Returning to 73's bed, Linda quietly replied.

"We would if we could. Don't worry! We'll make further inquiries tomorrow, but for now we must leave."

"Before the witch returns with her storm-troopers," said Bill, looking closely at the door half expecting her to charge through surrounded by massive security guards.

Linda witnessed 73's eyes slowly filling with tears as they were moving to leave, and it was all she could do to stop herself following suit. The sadness of this frail figure lying helpless before them tugged deeply at her heart. He lay staring at the ceiling, there wasn't a thing they could do for the moment, except give him hope about tomorrow and how they would move heaven and earth to get him away from Ward Six and hopefully the hospital. The camera installed earlier had been left running and they were hopeful the nurses didn't realize that it was motion-sensitive and would go on recording long into the night.

Chapter 8

Making their way cautiously back to the car along the narrow corridors with the sensation of hidden eyes burning deep upon their person, Bill and Linda felt most uncomfortable. The stench of anaesthetic lingered heavily in the air from each room passed as the sounds of suffering escaped from behind the curtains surrounding beds in the larger public wards.

"Linda! What was said back there?" whispered Bill, stopping dead in the middle of the corridor holding her gently by the arm, a blank look on his face.

"He claimed he was FBI and they were trying to silence him."

"Who were?"

"I guess the FBI. He mentioned the name Podgy!"

"Podgy! What self-respecting FBI agent would answer to the name Podgy?" replied Bill, smiling broadly.

"I think he said Podgy," said Linda. "Right now, I'm not sure. He spoke really slow, as though guarding his words. Either doesn't trust us, or he can't fully comprehend, perhaps due to the drugs they're filling him with. Even the advanced stage of the virus wouldn't be helping."

"What would an FBI agent be doing in Ward Six, and why is anyone trying to silence him? He may be delirious," said Bill.

"Perhaps, but I don't think so. I have this deep uncertain feeling there's more to it!" replied Linda.

"Like what?" asked Bill, having problems keeping up with her pace as she moved hurriedly through the corridor?

"Call it a hunch," she said, both of them bursting quickly out of the main doors and moving down the twelve steps to the car park below. Approaching their vehicle, a plain blue Ford with foreign number plates rapidly sped off, spraying the parked cars with loose gravel from the edge of the road. Out of the corner of his eye, Bill caught the flash of a camera from the person in the passenger seat.

"Who the hell was that?" gasped Linda, the Ford passing within inches of her.

"Good question! And why the camera?" replied Bill, his eyes focused on the Ford as it sped recklessly through the traffic, narrowly missing patients, hospital staff and a pregnant woman pushing her pram leisurely through the maze of parked cars.

"What are you talking about?" asked Linda, for she had been too occupied in getting out of the path of the rampaging car, too busy to notice anything unusual about the occupants of the speeding vehicle.

"Someone in that car had a camera, and it was focused directly at us!" was Bill's reply

"This is crazy," replied Linda, sliding the key into the lock and slowly opening the door, half expecting the car to burst into flames. "Why is this happening?"

"Your guess is as good as mine," said Bill. "But I'll bet my bottom dollar there's more to this than meets the eye. For some strange reason, by you talking to 73 we seem to have unleashed his demons. But the question remains! Why?"

Sitting quietly, their car moving slowly through the crowded parking area with only the radio breaking the silence, Linda pondered the reality of the situation, trying patiently to come to a realistic conclusion.

Why would anyone be trying to silence a dying AIDS sufferer? she thought. *Why wouldn't the hospital allow them to move 73 to a private room? Why only set hours per day to monitor the patient? What was the secrecy?*

The questions running through her mind made no sense, yet things were happening that defied all logic.

Chapter 9

Back at the safety of her apartment, Linda made coffee while Mick and Bill worked on the possibility of helping 73 away from Ward Six, maybe, with an ounce of luck, even from the hospital.

"Kidnapping!" said Mick, half turning to Linda who was standing by the large bay window looking down at the empty street below, her cup held gently in two hands as her hips swayed slowly to the music playing quietly in the background.

"If we have to, Mick you should have seen him. He's so helpless. He needs help and he needs it now," replied Linda, emotion quivering softly in her voice.

"But kidnapping, that's fairly outrageous for you two," said Mick with a half smile reappearing in the corner of his mouth.

"Why?" replied Linda, frowning at Mick's expression and moving to the coffee pot.

"Never mind, I like it. This could be really informative. And besides we owe these assholes something," Mick said, rubbing his hands vigorously together as Linda topped up his cup.

"What happened in the computer?" asked Bill purposely changing the subject.

"Nothing, the entire level you were after has been surgically erased," replied Mick now standing beside Linda looking down to the street, his arm cupped around her shoulders.

"Erased surgically, what do you mean by that?" asked Bill half knowing the answer.

"Bill, someone is selectively deleting all the files that have anything to do with past FBI missions between '68 and '74," said Linda. "Also, all names associated with the Firm in San Francisco during that period have either been changed or deleted."

"Do you have any idea what's missing?" said Bill.

"No! But whoever is clearing out the computer, is doing an excellent job," replied Mick.

"Again we've drawn a blank," said Linda, her expectations growing slimmer with each passing moment.

"Hopefully the people involved think so!" replied Mick, excitement written all over his face.

"What do you mean by think so?" replied Bill, hoping for an enlightening answer. "The level I was searching had all but been cleared while I was scanning, then somehow I stumbled into a program written years ago calling itself The Messiah."

"The Messiah!" exclaimed Linda. "What the hell's that?"

"Linda, haven't you read the Bible? The Messiah was Jesus Christ, son of God, put upon Earth to point us in the right direction!" said Mick sarcastically.

"Don't be a smart ass! What I meant is that why would anyone call a program The Messiah?" snapped Linda.

""I haven't the faintest! Somehow the decoder opened a new level. I don't even know if I can repeat the accident and get back in!" replied Mick.

"Interesting," said Bill. "Anything useful to our story?"

"The fingerprints you asked me to match are those of Carlos Rodriguez. He was an FBI operative who vanished in '87, presumed murdered by the drug lords of Columbia."

"That fits roughly with what he told me at the hospital," replied Linda.

"What's this?" asked Mick, following Linda across the room to where Bill was seated comfortably on the plush sofa, white flakes of paint still evident in his hair .

"What 73 told me at the hospital? I'll fill you in later," replied Linda. "By the way, if we're caught searching their computer, we could face twenty years."

"Relax," said Mick. "I was only in there a couple of minutes. Not enough time to run a back trace. Besides, I can't see any other way to help your story."

"He's right. We simply don't have a choice!" said Bill

"Linda, to ease your mind, I entered the central computer via a myriad of computers. To trace my entry, they would first have to trace at least half a dozen other entries throughout the world. Even with the best and unlimited manpower, that exercise would take no less than twenty minutes."

"Ok, I believe you," she replied, brushing the visible white flakes from Bill's hair.

"We still have to be extremely careful," said Mick. "But believe me, I wouldn't do anything to upset the Fed's. They hammered me some years ago when I was just starting out."

Feeling comfortable with Mick's explanation and elevated by his progress through the computer, they decided to have a small celebration at the quiet little restaurant around the corner and over dinner, plan the rescue of their patient from Ward Six.

Chapter 10

The next morning a letter was hand delivered to the out desk of the *Courier*. The letter was addressed to Linda McAllister and was to be opened only by her.

Linda, while driving to meet Bill at the hospital was interrupted by her mobile phone.

"Linda, I have a letter addressed to you!" came the voice over the phone in its rack on the dashboard.

"Alice, would you mind reading it to me?" replied Linda. "I'm already a half an hour late and the traffic wasn't doing me any favours."

"I can't Linda! It says obviously for your eyes only," replied Alice.

"I'll swing bye and pick it up! Thanks," said Linda as she disconnected the mobile phone.

She drove slowly through the early traffic pondering about their plan to rescue 73 from Ward Six and who in hell would deliver a letter to the *Courier* for her eyes only? In her own view she wasn't that important but was sure that the letter would make for some interesting reading. Parking illegally outside the office building, she raced up to her floor to be met by Alice who handed her the letter.

"Thanks Alice!" said Linda as she hurriedly made her way to the front of the foyer with Alice.

"Aren't you going to open it?" asked Alice.

"When I have time! I'm running a bit late as usual and I really must get my butt out of gear. I have to meet Bill early at the hospital," replied Linda, smiling as she exited the front doors.

"Can't he wait?" Alice yelled back, following Linda to the front door.

"No!" came the reply from Linda who had turned back to answer Alice's question. "This story is too important. I really must run. Again thank you and we'll catch up over lunch some time."

Linda raced back to the car that had been double parked, a parking ticket tucked neatly beneath the wiper blade. She swore softly and tucked the ticket in her bag.

Arriving at the hospital at the start of visiting hours, she could not help but hear the lingering sirens emanating in the background from the emergency wards at the other end of the building. People mingled with confusion throughout the different corridors, trying desperately to locate their loved ones. Linda seated in the wheel chair they had borrowed from her grandmother, wearing her long dark wig felt uncomfortable with the situation. Bill was waiting for her.

"Bill, I've had second thoughts," said Linda. "If we fail now, we won't get a second chance."

"Linda, we discussed all this last night!"

"I know, but now the plan seems stupid."

"Being so weak, he'll need the chair. We can't just carry him out. And as you saw, he's much too sick to walk" said Bill, annoyed that she was questioning last night's well laid plan. Although not entirely original, their goal was simple. In and out before anyone realized he was missing, and more importantly, with no-one getting hurt in the process.

"OK, let's do it," she replied, still unconvinced.

Quietly they made their way towards Ward Six, but on entering, their worst fears were realized. The old bed occupied earlier by 73 was now empty, made up ready to receive the next patient. It was as though he hadn't existed. Even the white paint flakes scattered throughout the ward had been painstakingly removed, leaving the highly polished floor reflecting the bright rays of sunlight, piercing through the tears and rips in the old blinds.

Not knowing what had transpired but realizing there was a problem, Bill asked Linda to remain in the chair and return directly to the car where he would join her in the blink of an eye, but not before finding out a few truths. As Linda disappeared down the narrow corridor, Bill moved to the nurses' station directly around the corner to inquire about 73's whereabouts.

Sister Karen Vincent, a close friend of the past few weeks, informed him of people arriving the night before and ordering the patient be transferred to Ward Nine, the maximum security area, with no visitation allowed.

"Why all this mystery, Karen?"

"William!" she exclaimed.

"Bill, please," he replied immediately.

"Bill, last night you would not have believed the security!"

"Why? Who was here?"

She paused, drew a deep breath while checking the corridors for prying eyes and it was only after she had satisfied herself that none were present, she answered his question.

"Admiral Rasmussen. The man is rude, arrogant and completely full of himself."

"Rasmussen? That name rings a bell. I'm sure someone wrote an article in the early seventies concerning his dissertations. And from memory, he's a dangerous bastard with the power behind him," replied Bill. *I wonder where he fits into this"* he thought to himself.

"Did you recognize anyone else? It's extremely important," he asked aloud.

"No! And come to think of it, the people with the Admiral didn't look like government agents or MPs, but what would I know!"

"Karen, is it possible to get to his ward undetected?"

"No."

"OK then. Where is Ward Nine in relation to where we are now?"

"It's on level five right next to maternity, next to the janitor's office. But I wouldn't go there if I were you. Bill the way it was last night, the confusion and yelling, these people will most certainly stop at nothing!"

"What about feeding and bathing? Who looks after that?"

"I don't know. Everyone was told in no uncertain terms to stay out of it," she replied, looking around nervously, making quite sure there was no chance of being overheard.

"Then who would I see about further interviews?"

"Bill, don't worry about it. No one here has that authority! Walk away, forget you were ever here."

"Karen! Why the turn around, why the change of heart, now that we finally got through to him?" Bill could see the nervousness in her movements, a condition he'd not witnessed earlier. She paused for what seemed an eternity before answering his question.

"That's the problem. He's awake and talking. No one anticipated this was going to happen. Bill I beg you. Please drop it!"

"Maybe you're right. Perhaps I'm making too much of this situation. It would be nice to have simple answers. But like I said, there are other immediate things to demand my attention" he said, sensing that Karen was warning him about the impending security cameras.

"Bill," she whispered, half turning her head from the camera. "This isn't normal hospital procedure!"

"I can see that," he replied. "I'm in no way blaming you. I'm upset it had to end this way. We feel deeply for 73."

"And I do, too!" she replied in a warm sympathetic response. "I have your mobile number. I'll call if the situation changes," she said, making Bill feel he owed her an apology.

"Thanks for all your help over these strained weeks. Somehow you've made this mess tolerable," he whispered, knowing that the people monitoring the security camera were still listening intently.

"My pleasure," she replied, giving Bill a huge hug as the buzzer and light sounded to room eleven. Hurriedly saying her last good-byes, she made her way down the corridor, around the corner and out of sight.

Chapter 11

Bill retrieved Mick's video gear stored neatly by the side counter but minus the cassette. He had the feeling it would be confiscated. An uneasy feeling had crept over him, making the hairs on the back of his neck uncomfortably upright. In the seconds since Karen had departed to answer her calling, adrenalin in his veins had started flowing freely and his heart was beating louder as he made his way towards the car where Linda waited patiently. She'd removed the wig and manoeuvred the mirrors in a way she could observe all exits leading from the hospital without turning her head. This way she remained anonymous making sure that when Bill finally exited the hospital, prying eyes weren't present and no-one was following.

"We'll that's it! End of the line," said Bill sliding in next to Linda.

"What do you mean, that's it?"

"I mean it's over! There's something here that we don't understand. And I think it's too dangerous to continue."

"What about him? Doesn't he matter? Linda replied angrily, pointing in the direction of his window.

"Sure he does! But there are forces involved here that we can't begin to comprehend. Linda, lets discuss this somewhere else. I still feel the presence of prying eyes," said Bill exiting the car-park, entering traffic with the feeling once more of "hopelessness" towards their story.

* * *

They arrived home to find Mick sitting on the stairs leading to Bill's and Mick's apartment with a look on his face that said it all.

"What's up? You look as though you've lost your best friend," said Linda, standing before him, the video camera draped loosely over her shoulder, her legs slightly apart and her ski hat pulled delicately down over her ears.

"We have a problem. While I was out some asshole trashed the apartment. They destroyed everything. The place is fucking totalled," replied Mick with anger, his eyes not leaving the pavement.

"Totalled," replied Linda moving next to Mick, her arm gently over his shoulder trying in a way to console his inner most feelings while removing the beanie and shaking her hair vigorously back into place.

"That's exactly what I said. The place has been broken into and ransacked!"

"What's going on? What have we done to upset whoever?" asked Linda.

"Mick, did you notice anything out of the ordinary when you returned besides the apartment being trashed?" asked Bill standing next to the others, looking at the offending apartment. The tall grey buildings on both sides of the street blotted out the sun as the cold north wind that had only started the night before tunnelled bitterly down the almost deserted streets, bending the young trees dotting the sidewalk, another failed attempt by the Mayor of San Francisco to restore nature to the central business district.

"There was a blue Ford parked suspiciously across the street with the guy in the passenger seat taking photos of yours truly and the surrounding buildings," replied Mick blowing gently into his cupped hands, trying in vain to put back some warmth and colour.

"The same thing happened to us in the car park of the hospital," said Linda.

"What are they after?" asked Mick, looking to Bill to provide some much needed answers.

"Why are you looking at me?" said Bill. "Perhaps they think we know something and they want to know what. I don't know!"

"Are you sure when you tapped into their computer you didn't disturb anyone in the Bureau?" asked Bill.

"Positive! There's no way. I was in only minutes."

"What about that other program, The Messiah?" asked Bill nervously.

"The FBI or CIA, I don't think they know the program exists."

"Can you be sure?" asked Linda.

"I can't be sure of anything! When I started downloading the computer, I didn't detect any form of scan. All areas in that level were clean."

"Well, somebody's upset someone," said Bill.

"What do you suppose they are looking for?" asked Linda, referring to the state of the apartment.

"Beats me, there's nothing missing except the photo we had taken of the three of us on our last ski trip to Aspen," replied Mick.

"That's a worry," said Bill. "Whoever they are, they now have our identity photos and we don't have a clue as to whom we are dealing with!"

"I think it's time we relocate," said Bill with his eyes looking to the spot where the offending Ford had been parked earlier.

"Meaning?" asked Linda, climbing the stairs to the apartment with the chilly north wind blowing her blonde hair across her face.

"Bill's saying if we decide to go back in the computer, we do so only from a public computer," was Mick's reply.

"You've lost me!" she replied brushing the offending hair back into place, the ice in the wind causing her cheeks to redden.

"Linda! Are you blonde?" asked Bill.

"Don't be a smart ass. It doesn't suit you!" she replied menacingly.

"If we enter the Central Computer and someone happens to get lucky and traces our entry, the trace will go directly to that computer. So by relocating, we'll not only safeguard our well being, but also make it extremely difficult for anyone to follow our trail. And by using computers via libraries all over San Francisco, if by some miracle they trace our entry, the entry will go to the last computer and logically by the time they react, we'll be long gone."

"Sounds more like a movie," said Linda.

"Sadly! But that's how it has to be," replied Mick.

"OK! Why go back in? I mean it sounds too dangerous," she replied, closing the door on the carnage, once their apartment.

"Ever since 73 woke from his coma and spoke to you, we've had a problem. I for one would like to find out exactly what that problem is!" replied Mick.

"Are you sure?" asked Bill, thumping his arms around his body trying in vain to stave off the bitter cold.

"Could also be fatal," replied Linda, tucking her arm gently around Bill searching for the warmth he carried.

"It could, but I for one need to know," replied Bill. "And besides, the only way to help your story is to find the truth. Whatever that may be!"

"Speaking of 73, how are we now going to help him?" Linda asked, again opening the door to the apartment.

"What's Linda talking about?" asked Mick, not knowing that 73 had been moved into top level security.

"They moved him from Ward Six to Ward Nine, with no visitations," replied Bill, entering the apartment.

"I was wondering what went wrong with last night's well thought out plan. It's strange," said Mick. "I feel something sinister lurking in the shadows. Something from the past, but I can't put a finger on the problem. It's an ominous feeling I've had for days, and now the apartment."

"Yeah, we've had the same feeling ever since the hospital, but we can't let feelings rule our thoughts! Not if we want to help 73," replied Bill.

"Mick, do you have you any problems with re-entering their computer and digging out all you can about 73?" asked Bill.

"Are you kidding? With or without you I'm going in. There is nothing on this planet that's going to stop me from finding out whom or what we are dealing with!"

"I thought that's what you would say. In that case we'll find someone game and smart enough to remove 73 from under their noses without anyone getting hurt!" said Bill.

"I know just the person," replied Linda, following Bill closely inside the apartment.

Chapter 12

A few days later, Linda rang Bill saying she'd located her friend and could she bring him over.

"Linda, where are you ringing from?" Bill asked.

"Home, why?" she replied.

"How about meeting me for lunch?"

"Bill, is something wrong? You sound worried!"

"Not really!" he said, not wanting to worry her. "It's just been a couple of days since I last saw you and I feel I owe you a lunch."

"A lunch where?"

"Tudor House, on Little and Strand, at two o'clock."

"Who's treating?" she asked, knowing that quite often Bill travelled light, without cash.

"What's this, forty questions? Mine, of course!" he said.

"Great!" she replied, hanging up the phone. Bill held on to hear the second click; he'd heard a similar sound earlier when she answered. Somehow her phone was tapped and he needed to know by whom. The trap had been set. Now it was time to find the truth and hopefully come up with a face.

* * *

Arriving at Linda's along the back streets in the hope of avoiding being followed, Bill entered quietly through the open security door. Linda, in a half state of dress heard the rear door close and as she wasn't expecting company, especially through the back, reached for the gun kept in her dresser. Moving discreetly from the bedroom, tiptoeing so as not to make a sound, she moved quickly to cover the hall and dining area. A silhouette appeared from the shadow, the light from behind making it impossible for her to see a face.

"Freeze or I'll shoot!" she yelled, holding the gun in the breached position taught to her by her father, pointing directly at the shadow standing in the darkened hall.

"Don't shoot! For Christ's sake, it's me, Bill," he yelled in a high pitched, panic-stricken tone, holding his arms high above his head.

"Bill is that you? What the hell are you doing here?" shouted Linda, her breathing gradually subsiding.

"Linda! Put the gun down," said Bill from the dark. "Of course it's me. You were expecting someone else?"

"Frankly, I wasn't expecting anyone. I thought we were supposed to meet for lunch!"

"You're phone's tapped. This was the only way I could think of to find out by whom," he replied sheepishly, moving out from the shadows and adjusting his tie, making his way towards her.

"Fucking men, dumb as dog shit!" she said quietly under her breath, heading towards the bedroom, stocking feet, pants and bra and the gun still clutched tightly in her hand.

"Did you say something?" he asked sheepishly, following her to the bedroom but keeping a safe distance.

"Do you always enter a woman's bedroom this way?"

"Sorry, I didn't mean to startle you. Cute ass," he said.

"I could have shot you dead," she replied angrily. "And leave my ass out of this."

"Yes, but you didn't. Sorry," he replied, sheepishly trying to answer her questions as they were being propelled at him.

"Bill, what am I going to do with you? Here, zip me up," she said, pulling into a tight blue dress that complimented every curve of her body. "Now, what's on your mind?" she asked, tugging things delicately into place.

"Could you make me out a woman? I mean from the waist up? I'll be seated in the car, so there'll be no need for stockings and high heels."

"Anything's possible. But the Mo will have to go," she replied, still showing signs of annoyance. "Why a woman or shouldn't I ask?"

"I want to drive past the restaurant to see who shows. And they wouldn't be expecting a couple of females."

"Could work," she replied. "But how will we know who we are looking for?"

"All we can look for is the Blue Ford. Hopefully they have let down their guard and use the same vehicle," replied Bill. "If not I don't know what to do," he said.

Bill sat quietly as Linda did her thing. He reflected on the amount of time the female sacrifices before the mirror, going through the routine rituals in order to entice the male. Adding the makeup, lipstick and perfume the general things that would drive a man crazy if roles were reversed. The moustache had gone and he felt quite naked, but a sacrifice had to be made. The wig Linda had selected felt uncomfortably tight and surprisingly heavy on his head. Not a feeling he fancied, so the sooner this was over, the better.

* * *

Driving slowly past Tudor House, the yuppies equivalent to a coffee shop with their foamy cappuccinos and creamy lattés, Bill started developing a feeling of paranoia. Was this all in his mind? Had he really heard the clicks? The doubts were flooding into his mind and Linda's attitude didn't help his disposition. Each time she glanced in his direction, she burst into open spontaneous laughter. The lipstick, rouge and especially the wig that he was wearing trying to look intelligent made for a comical situation.

"Look! The Ford parked down the alley," quipped Bill, finally wiping the smile from Linda's face.

"Why are they doing this? What have we done? Who are they?" asked Linda, more to herself than to Bill.

"Shit! The tint on the windows is so heavy I can't make out the silhouette figure seated behind the wheel," said Linda squinting to get a better view.

"Neither can I," said Bill adding to their confusion.

"Doesn't matter," said Linda. "We have a plate! And we know now that these are the same people that we crossed in the car-park." She smiled like a Cheshire cat as they moved slowly through the heavy traffic, the midday sun radiating the glorious heat of a warm spring day, a far cry from the cold blustery winds of days earlier.

"You're a sweetie. I'll get Mick to run a check on the plates," replied Bill with a touch of satisfaction then looking back one last time at the Ford parked inoffensively by the curb.

"Speaking of Mick, where is he these days?" she asked quietly.

"He's being kept busy visiting libraries!" replied Bill.

"So he's into it?" she asked.

"As we discussed earlier, they're computer-linked and extremely public. Exactly the safety we need to make sure nobody gets hurt," said Bill.

"And you don't think he may get caught?" she asked.

"Give him credit. He's good at his trade. Besides, we're meeting him for dinner at Bluey's. Perhaps he will have some enlightening information about 73 and hopefully the assholes we are dealing with."

Chapter 13

Bluey's was only a small diner bar, mostly used by locals, hardly ever a stranger entering. The food, though not exotic, was always plentiful, with everything except the ice cream cooked lovingly in a thick garlic marinade by the big man himself. The barmaids who worked there were all ex-hookers or strippers who had fallen on hard times or become too old for their profession, but now helping create this unique and attractive place. A three-piece band played every night, the songs of yesterday and at ten o'clock a talent quest was held, very popular, with the patrons at the bar throwing money at the hopefuls.

"You have to meet Dusty?" Linda said.

"He dug up most of the ground work at the Weekly before retiring, but still helps dad out occasionally when things get tough," added Linda, a smile gleaming on her face and the expectation in her voice making her seem almost child-like.

"Linda, I would prefer someone wearing a younger man's clothes. I don't like the thought of involving a geriatric in something I'm not sure of!"

"Bill, I assure you, Dusty's no geriatric," Linda replied with force.

"He's retired, isn't he? Linda, will you stop? I'm trying to be serious," he said, both smiling and frowning.

"I can't. Not until you shave your legs," she replied glancing at his hairy pegs crossed as a female and again bursting into laughter. The look on Bill's face sitting in the passenger seat endeavouring to be serious, wearing the lipstick, rouge, wig with a false bra and the hairy legs had become too much.

"Bill, if you don't like Dusty when you meet, there won't be a problem," she said, tears of laughter now streaming freely down her cheeks.

"Give a guy a break," said Bill, unable to look in her direction for fear of more ridicule.

Slowly they made their way back to her apartment where Bill changed into his civvies and discarded the makeup and wig, feeling quite humbled by his experience.

"See you tonight, sweetie. Cute ass," she laughed, her wolf whistle ringing loudly throughout the room as he quietly closed the door before heading for the safety and dignity of home.

Chapter 14

That night, Bill arrived at Bluey's bar early. He needed desperately to confer with Wendy, his main source of information from the streets. He moved through the crowded bar, the smell of stale tobacco lingering thick in the air with a young patron passed out across the counter, his beer grasped tightly in hand. He heard the cheerful sound of working girls laughing aloud from the booth opposite, striving to draw attention to their cause, but falling on deaf ears. Sitting discreetly at the end of the bar observing the good times being had, he was soon joined by Wendy.

"Hi gorgeous, any word on the streets?" asked Bill as Wendy, with her long slender legs well displayed by her tiny skirt lowered herself onto the adjoining stool, the lights from behind the bar shimmering softly through her long dark hair. She was wearing a see-through blouse, highlighted by her unusually square shoulders and her elbow length gloves. Wendy was tall but painfully thin, carrying her posture as a super model, even though the closest she'd come to a modelling career had been the catwalk at junior high. Heads turned wherever she went, a gesture she quietly enjoyed.

"What word, William?" She loved calling him William, and had done so since their early years in school.

"Wendy, why William, when you know I prefer Bill?" he frowned then smiled. The barman approached and Bill ordered a scotch with a white wine for Wendy, her tastes well known to him since their youth.

"With Linda, you're Bill! With me, you're William. That way I'm not crossing her turf."

Must be female logic, he thought to himself, though he couldn't understand the reasoning, and then repeated his question.

"Is there any word on the street about us?"

"Us?" she repeated, looking puzzled.

"Linda, Mick and myself," replied Bill, peering through the smoke at her slender body mounting the barstool, facing him with not a care, her legs distractingly apart.

"No, nothing William, why, is something wrong?" she replied as Bluey behind the bar approached, sweat rolling from his brow, dripping through the thick chest hair protruding from the off-white singlet he wore.

"Everything to your satisfaction, Bill?" he asked in his friendly, familiar tone.

"Yes, couldn't be better," replied Bill politely, with Wendy holding on tight to his arm, her foot gently caressing the inner part of his leg. "Just waiting on Linda and Mick."

"You're a gamer man than I," replied Bluey, smiling as he left them alone.

"What do you suppose he meant by that?" asked Bill.

"I think he's worried that there's something between us, with Linda possible only minutes away."

"Isn't it bizarre? Everyone thinks that Linda and yours truly are an item. I would love that to be so, but I think that she has other ideas."

"William you guys are soul mates. It's a union made in heaven. Even if you or she can't see it, the rest of the world can," replied Wendy smiling as she taunted his male ego.

Just as Wendy completed her sentence, a tall grey-haired stranger heavily tanned with character lines entrenched deeply onto his face entered the bar through the kitchen accompanied by Linda.

"Hi Bill, Wendy, I'd like you to meet my good friend Dusty," said Linda, squeezing her body in between them.

"Linda speaks very highly of you," replied Bill, shaking Dusty's large hand, its enormous power gently held back, a gesture Bill greatly appreciated.

"And what's your relationship to Linda?" asked Bill as he stood beside her looking up at the big man towering over him.

There was a quiet for a moment. Then the big man slowly spoke.

"I held her when she was born. I held her when she was christened. I'm still holding her and I will till the day I die" answered Dusty in his gravelly voice reflecting untold loyalty. "Does that answer your question?"

"I wasn't prying sir!" replied Bill now finding it hard to swallow.

"I'm glad," said the big man smiling at Linda.

"Gentlemen, I think Bluey wants me to mingle, but I'll be back," said Wendy, with Dusty standing in a gentlemanly gesture. "I see chivalry is not dead," she said, then moved quickly to the other end of the bar, a passing wink in leaving.

"Where the hell's Mick?" asked Linda, ordering a round of drinks for the trio.

"Don't know. He should be here," replied Bill with Mick entering the bar right on the time of lock-up.

Lock-up was the time when all doors were bolted shut as the small bell on the bar sounded eight. Those who were in were in, with no further entries of patrons for the night, a custom that had been implemented years ago when Bluey first purchased the bar. It assured those who wanted the exclusive night, arrived early, with no exceptions!

A remarkably beautiful young woman approached the group and stood close to Dusty who smiled and put his arm round her tiny waist.

"This is Grace, my best and favourite hostess," said Dusty

"Care to be seated?" asked Grace politely, leading the trio to an exclusive private booth, Bluey's personal pride and joy, with her perfume lingering a slight hint of musk long after she had departed.

"Sorry I'm late," puffed Mick hastily, sliding in next to Linda, pecking her lovingly on the cheek, a quaint brother-to-sister gesture.

"Mick, I'd like you to meet Dusty," said Bill but Mick didn't answer. Instead he saluted with his left hand from the darkened side of the booth while pulling out loose pages from his briefcase.

"I do believe you've upset some powerful people," said Dusty in his distinctive voice.

"Quite possibly, but I can't see how, or who," replied Mick.

"Hopefully I can help," said Dusty. His rugged features and awesome size made Mick feel comfortable this man was on their side.

"How did everything go at the library?" asked Bill while pouring himself a beer as the next round arrived.

"Libraries!" repeated Mick. "I've been to all nine. Not wanting to linger too long in one place."

No one answered, but Dusty nodded a form of approval as he sipped slowly from his glass.

"Are you going to tell us? Or do we have to guess?" asked Linda inquisitively, picking the fresh green olive from her glass and placing it tantalizingly in her mouth.

"Easy girl! Let the little guy gather his thoughts. After all we have all night and we don't want to jump to conclusions" said Dusty making a gesture with his hand for Mick to continue.

"Thank you, sir!" answered Mick while still pulling loose pages from his briefcase on the table before him.

"Things have strangely come in two parts! First, when I ran the finger print check on 73, I ended up with the name Carlos Rodriguez. Now he was the right-hand man to J. Edgar Hoover in the early and late sixties, executed supposedly by the drug lords of Columbia back in '87. The entire event had been witnessed and recorded by Hamish Wallace, who was at the time was with the New York Times."

"And part two?" asked Linda, ordering herself another martini from a passing waiter.

"Here's the problem! A code, a cryptic mess, that I can see no way of breaking. It shouldn't even be there," replied Mick as Wendy with her drink in hand cheerfully rejoined the group slipping in next to Dusty.

"To tell you the truth, I have no idea where this is leading. The code defies all logic I'm entirely in the dark," replied Mick, a person who hated not being in control of the computer, with the word "can't" not being in his vocabulary.

"What has J. Edgar Hoover to do with anything?" asked Linda, continuing to suck the olive, seductively rolling the seed between her lips.

"I don't know! But I intend to find out," replied Mick, smiling at Linda from the darkened corner of the booth.

"Can you recognize anything in this cryptic mess?" asked Dusty, looking down at Wendy's legs protruding from beneath the table.

"Sorry!" replied Mick, half-embarrassed at his failure to come to terms with the code, at the same time pouring himself another glass of champagne.

"I'd like to contact a close friend of mine. Robert Muller," said Dusty.

"Who's he?" asked Mick.

"Robert is the director of the FBI. I thought perhaps his people could be of assistance," replied Dusty, his eyes removed from Wendy's loins, now observing the patrons at the bar.

"What if they're the ones giving us a hard time?" asked Linda, looking up into the big man's eyes.

"That only happens in movies," he replied, placing a reassuring hand on her shoulder. "Besides Bobby is a close friend. He wouldn't do anything out of line to discredit his office."

"I'd like to know where J. Edgar fits into this mess," said Bill, sipping slowly from his glass of beer.

"Worse! Why is an FBI person in Ward Nine and denied help?" replied Linda, confused as the rest.

"Are we sure he's FBI?" asked Bill.

"Fingerprints don't lie," replied Mick.

"All right then! Who died in Columbia, and why is Carlos in the advanced AIDS ward of San Francisco Central? And why is the FBI supposedly trying to silence him?" asked Linda.

"I don't know! And there's no way this fucking code is going to tell me," replied Mick with his inner frustrations beginning to take their toll. "The only person capable of answering their questions was Carlos."

It became essential to the group that they talk to Carlos and also contact Hamish Wallace to see what light he may shed on the subject. With business concluded, Linda while looking into her handbag for her touch up lipstick came across the letter she had received yesterday but had failed to open.

"What's in the letter?" asked Bill as he poured himself another drink.

"I don't know! The letter was mysteriously hand delivered to the Courier yesterday morning and addressed to me personally," she replied while tearing open the envelope.

"Well show us!" said Mick hoping the letter might add some light on the code.

"It's a friend!" said Linda looking to the back of the letter.

"Linda just read it out loud so we can all be involved," said Dusty looking at Linda to hurry up.

The letter started; *To Linda McAllister, you don't know me and you probably never will as we are not destined to meet. The person in Ward Six is of significant importance to you and your story. Believe what he has to say without question, although at times what he says may not make a great deal of sense. Together we have been to hell and back and it's not right what they have done to him. If I hadn't disappeared when I did, I would have suffered the same fate. The people you are dealing with are desperate to suppress the truth. They are very powerful and extremely dangerous and will stop at nothing. In today's world they don't even exist. I will further enlighten you as you unravel the truth but be ever so careful - A friend.*

The letter was written in wobbly hand and if one read between the lines the author's pain was palpable.

"Well that tears it! Now we have to get 73 if what I suspect and he is still alive, he won't be for long," said Dusty looking at the faces around him.

The group decided that Dusty would endeavour to find Hamish. Linda and Bill were to speak to Carlos and somehow remove him from Ward Nine and in the process, convince the people lurking in the shadows that they were not a threat and only wanted to do a story about the despair of the AIDS sufferers around the world.

Feeling good about the night and forgetting their troubles they dined, danced and sang well into the wee hours, the three-piece band pumping out the tunes of a bygone era, songs they had grown up with, the lyrics of yesteryear.

Chapter 15

The following morning, Bill rang the hospital early asking to speak to Sister Karen Vincent to arrange a visit with patient 73 and hopefully broaden their research into his condition. Nurse Wilson who answered the phone said in a deep authoritative voice that Sister Vincent who had previously worked there, had yesterday afternoon been transferred to the isolated Naval base hospital located on the northern outskirts of San Francisco Bay. He then asked about patient 73 and if possible could he arrange an informal meeting to enquire further about his condition.

"I'm sorry," the nurse replied. "He passed away late last night from AIDS-related complications."

"He's dead!" gasped Bill, feeling the uncertainty of loss.

"Yes! And with no known family, the hospital has arranged to have the body cremated immediately."

Isn't that a bit quick? he thought to himself, but didn't elaborate as he knew it wouldn't get him anywhere.

"I thank you for your help," he replied, hiding his frustration, but the uncertainty intermittently swelled him with anger.

"Not a problem," she replied.

Bill was sure that she was quietly laughing at his feeble attempts to contact a patient and her in complete control.

Nothing that had happened or was happening made any sense! Now someone would have to enter the hospital to find the truth. Even if their worst fears were realized they somehow had to know! Bill had only just hung up the phone when it rang.

"Bill, could you meet me at the 42nd Street Library?" came Mick's voice. They felt safe again, as Mick had earlier found the bug and removed it to a public phone.

"What's happening?" inquired Bill, wondering what Mick had discovered, but there was no reply. The phone had gone dead.

* * *

Bill arrived at the library, a huge daunting building erected almost seventy years ago displaying all the splendour of the Renaissance. Thirty three steps packed with students led to the entrance, a journey he did not want to undertake, but go he must.

Walking down the huge marble corridors, he kept hearing the echoing silence that belonged to this house of learning. The sound of his footsteps echoed along the hallway, at times almost deafening. Trying extremely hard not to attract attention, he found himself tip-toeing through the main arch and on to the computer section where Mick was seated by the main computer deeply engrossed in what he was doing, completely lost to the situation.

"What's so important it couldn't wait?" asked Bill. "And why did you hang up on me?"

"I didn't. My phone shit itself!" answered Mick in a half whisper, his eyes newer leaving the screen. Leaning over, Bill saw that the screen displayed a map of the Caribbean area.

"Shush!" came the sound from the woman seated opposite, her wire rimmed glasses blending perfectly with her glowing red lipstick, taking Bill by surprise as he caught her eye.

"Sorry," replied Bill quietly.

"Look!" whispered Mick pointing to a small isle on the screen. "That's Haiti."

"Isle of golden sands and beautifully tanned women," replied Bill, half dreaming of the brochures he had seen at the local travel agency just around the corner from the apartment.

"Also the poorest country in the world," said Mick.

"Sorry, I'm getting too far ahead without explaining myself," said Bill.

"The Virus!" said Mick. "It's a monkey disease, recorded over a thousand years throughout Haiti. I think something here relates to aids. But not the monkey version of the virus we know today." He tapped his notes nervously.

"What do you mean? What are you actually saying?" asked Bill in a whisper.

"If I knew I'd tell you. But there is something wrong with the whole situation. It starts off telling us about the AIDS in the baboons of Haiti. Then it concludes with the human version of the virus."

"I'm still not clear as to what you're getting at!" said Bill.

"Before the cryptic code took over, there was information about the baboons of Haiti. There was also two dates and I don't know how they connect," replied Mick, with confusion etched deep into his face.

"What of Carlos?" asked Bill.

"He's the one making the entry. Look here. Mick pointed to the top left of the screen. "He gives three names, Hoover, Ramos and Prodi."

"Shush!" came again.

Bill merely looked at the woman before she upped and moved.

"Can you make sense of anything?" asked Bill.

"Not really. But Carlos somehow warns about Haiti. And to watch out!" replied Mick.

"For what?" asked Bill.

"Don't know," replied Mick. "He also refers to J. Edgar 'The instigator,' whatever that means."

"Instigator of what?"

The 'shushes' were now ringing out from all areas of the library. So engrossed had they become in the computer, their voices had steadily climbed to normal.

"That's where I lose it. There the cryptic starts and there's no cross-reference," whispered Mick, carefully sliding back into the chair, staring blankly at the screen.

"Then what the hell am I doing here?" asked Bill quietly.

"Bear with me. I need an impartial mind. I don't want to end up with tunnel vision," replied Mick, moving forward and enlarging part of the screen.

"Before the code starts, the word 'baboon' appears frequently, followed closely by 'virus,'" he continued. "Then down here," pointing to the lower part of the screen, "it looks like 'Zaire' and on the next line the first date, April 10 1970, but that could be my assumption."

"I'm amazed that you can make anything of this crap!" whispered Bill. He pointed at a couple of lines lower down. "What's this?"

"That's the second date. September 14 1970, followed closely by San Francisco," replied Mick.

"San Francisco 1970! What does that suggest?" asked Bill.

"Haven't a clue! Also this reference to Hoover Private," said Mick.

"Hoover Private? Now that rings a bell," said Bill. "Can you enhance that?"

Mick quickly punched the required keys. "What has the institute to do with anything?" he asked.

"The Hoover Institute of Advanced Research and Technology," said Bill. He paused, searched the library for prying eyes, and then quietly under his breath answered Mick's question.

"In the late sixties and early seventies, J. Edgar and a few of his trusted lieutenants in the FBI used the Hoover Institute of Advanced Research and Technology for what was to be believed their own means. Nothing that went on inside was ever released to the public. All information required by the press was classified under the National Securities Act, locked away for the next seventy years, protecting the bastards!"

"Well, shit!" said Mick.

"Can only happen in America," muttered Bill, searching the screen for more enlightening answers.

"Yeah, God Bless America," replied Mick.

"What do you mean by that?" asked Bill.

"Simply, God Bless America!" said Mick sarcastically.

"I remember vividly the institute burning to the ground," said Bill. "But nothing about how the fire started, or if there was any loss of life. Everything associated with the hospital was conveniently swept under the carpet." Bill shook his head in disbelief.

"Don't you find it strange that it never made the headlines, even way back then?" whispered Mick, his eyes busily flashing along the screen.

"With the bastards they had running it and the people in power, no I don't!" answered Bill, his eyes still searching the library.

"Mick, let's get out of here. Now!" replied Bill, noticing a large man in a dark suit seated at the other end of the library, an open book on the table in front of him, but studying their conversation closely, his eyes staring directly at them. Another person was to their left, her red dress glaringly obvious as she stood out from the crowd, her eyes directly focused on their computer.

Was this the same woman he'd seen at the hospital, or was he now becoming obsessed? thought Bill.

"Wait a minute, there has to be something we've missed," replied Mick, oblivious to Bill's pleas. "We definitely need Carlos."

"Mick, come on," repeated Bill as the man in the dark suit had somehow vanished from sight. And the woman was no longer in the library, but how could she have passed by them without him noticing? The only way out was past their computer and she had definitely not come their way.

Bill's innermost fears rose up in his mind. Childhood fears, a child stalked by a stranger when he was only seven, the memory of the ordeal burned deep into his soul and his fears felt the same. Fears that he no longer wanted to realize.

"I have some shit news," said Bill, his thoughts flashing back to the present then he told Mick about his earlier conversation with the nurse about how Carlos had suddenly passed away and his remains directly cremated.

"For argument's sake, let's say Carlos is dead. How the hell are we going to put anything together?" asked Bill, his eyes still searching the corners of the library, looking for prying eyes, the nerve ends towards the back of his neck craving immediate attention.

"I've extracted a bogus name from their computer I think could be the sister to Carlos. But she lives in Puerto Prince, Haiti."

"What's her name?" asked Bill his eyes still scouring the corners of the library searching for the woman in red.

"Her name is Peta Maria Santos. Perhaps she could be of help."

"You're a genius!" yelled Bill, his voice echoing loudly throughout the library, standing ready to leave as he grabbed Mick by the arm with one hand, the other slamming the shutdown key to the computer.

"What's going on?" asked Mick as he was dragged from the computer.

"I'll tell you when we get home!" answered Bill happy to see the end of the library and hopefully the people monitoring their conversation.

* * *

Mick laboured for days at the computer using the decoder, setting and resetting, but to no avail. He couldn't match the code.

"What's happening?" asked Linda arriving only minutes earlier, her slim body dressed in the psychedelic colours of the sixties.

"There's no fucking way!" Mick replied, looking Linda straight in the eye, bursting into laughter.

"Linda! The hippie look?" smiled Mick then bursting into open laughter.

"Explain yourself," she replied with annoyance.

"Never mind," he replied, smiling cautiously, knowing this was something to stay well clear of. "Don't ever tell a female she's dressed wrong!

Chapter 16

The time had come to gather everyone together, to pool their knowledge and try to find out where things were heading and maybe resolve some of the mystery surrounding their story.

Alexander Falls, a small private cabin owned by the magazine only forty miles due east of the city, serenely guarded by rolling hills backing to a beautiful pale blue private lake seemed the perfect answer. Linda had spent countless months there in her youth and as such knew every blade of grass for miles around, a comforting thought in light of the situation. People unknown to them, for some reason following their every move, tapping telephones, taking pictures from speeding cars and ruthlessly destroying apartments, all this definitely called for drastic measures.

Howard had brought with him enough provisions to feed a small army and Dusty had somehow located Hamish, convincing him to attend their small gathering. Mick had with him the data gathered from the central computer, including the pages of code he'd laboured deep into many a night to break.

Things had not always gone well, so now it was time to relax and unwind, let their hair down and enjoy each other's company and above all, to swap any available information no matter how trivial and try to extract some logic from the situation.

Midday, and the weather warmed to a beautiful sunny day with the lake a pale colour of green, turning a deeper shade of blue towards the middle. A tiny waterfall trickled quietly in the distance, winding its way from high in the hills to the calm and refreshing pond below. The wildlife in the area bordered on abundant. Deer grazed on meadows of grass, looking like wheat swaying gracefully in the breeze, adding to the peace and serenity offered by the lake. A small landing at the rear of the cabin made for some excellent fishing and with countless rocking chairs scattered around, they settled to the quiet of the valley.

Dusty had with him the son and daughter of his late friend, Chief Little Wolf. Nathan, though not the largest American Indian, had been raised in the tradition of the Apache. His sister Saara who was almost nineteen had been brought up living in New York with her mother, but was now trying to recapture her Indian heritage.

The warmth of the afternoon became too inviting for the young ones. Nathan, his tanned body with muscles rippling with youth went swimming with Saara. Her long shiny black hair covered her youthful breasts, hiding the modesty women of the twenty first century exploit. Wearing a G-string, which hardly covered her made it impossible for anyone to concentrate on the matters at hand. Not that anyone really wanted to.

The day passed quickly as everyone relaxed, watching the young ones swimming in the clear crystal waters with the warm breeze of the afternoon whipping up a chop towards the centre of the lake. Mick and Linda, unable to resist any longer joined them, diving in fully-clothed to the sound of laughter echoing loudly around the hills, the deer and the other creatures leisurely stopping to share their precious moment.

* * *

Nightfall had arrived and with dinner past, Nathan and Saara at Dusty's request moved discreetly outside. Bill complimented Howard on a wonderful meal, cooked by his own skilful hands, hands that had been taught the art of a chef by his ex-wife over the fifteen year period they had been married.

Howard, seated at the head of the table, was puffing on a dollar cigar, a wisp of garlic lingered still, so when Dusty lit his pipe it became time to open a window. The night had turned cool, a touch of mist rose slowly from the lake and with the wind easing the waters became cold beneath the full moon, occasionally ducking behind lineal clouds racing across the darkened sky. When the crickets fell quiet and the waterside frogs started their song, Bill somehow felt a calm he hadn't known since he knew not when.

"Why all this mystery?" started Howard, breaking the stillness of the quaint little log cabin, warmed by the old black potbelly stove in the corner.

"You've come to me asking to write a story about the compassionate side of AIDS. Well that's OK. But now I find my old friend Dusty and these two young people, Nathan and Saara involved in what?" He was going to continue, but somehow Mick slipped under his guard, interrupting in a soft voice.

"Howard, we called this gathering because I suspect we've somehow stumbled onto someone's dark secret!" he said. "Something that happened in the sixties and it involves Hoover and the institute of technology."

"Someone's secret! And what might that be?" asked Howard, a hint of sarcasm in his voice. He didn't want or need his time being wasted.

"If it's what we suspect, and there's so much we don't know, the people responsible couldn't afford this going public," replied Mick, looking to Linda for support while placing the computer sheets next to Howard's outstretched hand.

"Cryptic! What the hell am I going to do with this?" Howard asked, puffing on his stogie, the remnants of the re-lit cigar with the smoke now lingering heavily in the room, but replaced by a tension so quiet, one could hear a pin drop.

"Dad, listen to what Mick has to say," said Linda, slightly annoyed by her father's interruptions.

"Sorry, sir here's a copy of the same papers partially decoded," said Mick.

"Why only partially decoded?"

"Because no matter how hard I try or what methods I use I can't break this bloody code," replied Mick, pointing to the papers held by Howard.

"Could it be that difficult?" asked Howard. Cynicism was not his usual expression as he was normally a person of extreme compassion and greater understanding, but now he was unsure.

"Dad!" interrupted Linda.

"I was merely asking the question. After all, I am paying the bills."

"Some," said Bill.

"OK some," Howard agreed.

"Howard this is extremely important," said Mick, his annoyance with the man becoming glaringly obvious.

"Where did you get your information?" asked Howard.

"The Central Computer," snapped Mick.

"The Central Computer, what the hell's that?" asked Howard staring at Mick.

"There's a level in their computer that shouldn't exist. I've never seen anything like it, not in all my years of breaking and delving into the files of the corporate giants. The level defies all logic."

"Are you talking Central as in Control?" asked Hamish quietly, listening, sipping from a small glass of port, unobtrusively grabbing everyone's attention.

"Yes, I am, sir," replied Mick politely.

"What the hell's going on? Could someone please enlighten an old man?" said Howard, the cigar smouldering in his hand.

"Central is the main computer in San Francisco linked directly to the head computer in Washington. Used exclusively by the combined forces," answered Hamish. "Army, Navy, Airforce, with some limited access given to NASA."

"What the fuck are we doing there?" asked Howard frowning.

"We're there because the FBI and CIA also use the computer. When Bill asked the authorities to run a fingerprint match on 73 it turned up negative. Yet earlier at the hospital, 73 told Linda he was FBI and they were trying to silence him."

"Is that true, Linda?"

"Yes Dad! But he spoke ever so softly. It was extremely difficult to make out exactly what he was saying."

"In other words you're not sure of what he said?" said Howard.

"No! But I'm positive he maintained that the FBI was trying to silence him," she replied.

"I'm sorry, Mick you have my undivided attention," replied Howard, finally putting down the cigar, much to everyone's delight.

"Thank you," said Mick, pausing to collect his thoughts. "Using the decoder I decided to conduct my own search," he continued. "But the level containing the information I was after had been cleared or being so as I searched. In desperation and great haste, I somehow stumbled into a program calling itself "The Messiah."

The room remained deadly quiet, only the occasional breeze outside breaking the silence of the cabin.

"You said earlier the program shouldn't be there?" asked Hamish, again sipping his port.

"Correct! Yet these pages of code are what I've extracted, along with names, dates and places," replied Mick, looking closely at the faces around him.

"And what names might they be?" asked Hamish.

"Names and dates and as far as I'm concerned they relate to nothing at least not in today's world. The inconsistencies just keep happening!" answered Mick.

"Try me on the names," said Hamish, refilling his glass while holding on tight to the bottle.

"Right, the first names to appear are those of Ramos and Prodi," replied Mick.

"Part of the old guard," said Hamish.

"Could someone clarify?" said Howard, leaning comfortably back in the chair, re-lighting the stub of his cigar.

"They were both FBI operatives in the late sixties, seventies and early eighties," said Hamish.

"From memory, the rumour was that in the early years, J. Edgar formed an elite squad to do his bidding. I believe there were three names, however the third name eludes me at the moment. Sorry, Mick, I was rambling, please continue."

"Don't apologize," replied Mick. "I'm grateful to have someone with knowledge of the people we're dealing with." He paused, collecting his thoughts, then continued. "Haiti, Baboon and Virus, with a reference to Zaire April 10 and San Francisco September 14 appear, also a random reference to the Hoover Private Institute."

"Hoover Private," interjected Hamish, again filling his glass from the nearly empty bottle. "For years I tried to interview J. Edgar about the rumours surrounding the institute. But I found the task beyond me."

"Why were you interested?" asked Linda.

"My younger brother James worked for the FBI at the time," said Hamish. "He was admitted to the hospital for minor exploratory surgery. He vanished without trace."

"Vanished?" said Howard. "It sounds a bit like that show, The X-Files."

"Worse! These people are for real," replied Hamish, continuing with his story. "Someone once told me that the Hoover Institute of Advanced Research and Technology was being used for private genetic experimentation. Whenever I established a meeting to interview the ones who worked there, I found they suddenly disappeared, were transferred or tragically killed in freak accidents."

"Didn't the authorities question the goings on?" asked Linda, moving comfortably closer to Hamish.

"They were the authorities, and not to be fooled with. That is, if you valued your existence."

"Are you telling me these people were murderers?" asked Linda.

"Absolutely, but I can't prove it," said Hamish. "Murder however, being their last option. J Edgar's people found more pleasure in discrediting anyone who crossed them. In those days so badly were some people victimised, that the White House with the Kennedys in power and all their influence, weren't game to cross the man."

He looked round the room. He had everybody's full attention.

"I'll give you another example," continued Hamish. "A young nurse in late '69 rang me one afternoon. Accidentally, she'd stumbled onto something, and was in grave fear of her life. I drove as fast as I could to her apartment, but sadly not quickly enough. Stepping from my car, I heard her scream. Someone had pushed her out the seventh floor window."

"How did you know she was pushed?" asked Mick softly.

"Cathryn was the type of girl who loved life. She wouldn't end her life that way, not by her own hand and knowing that I was only minutes away."

"You're kidding!" said Linda badly shaken by Hamish's revelations.

"I wish I was! And sadly, there was never any evidence to incriminate the bastards."

"What was it she stumbled on?" asked Howard.

"We only talked briefly, but the one thing she did mention was that a Doctor Farnsworth from England had somehow genetically changed a new virus that he was working on. He was trying to coat that virus with the body's own sugar molecules! To this day I'm still not sure what she meant, but it may be a good idea to find out!" replied Hamish with tears swelling up in his eyes.

"A sugar coated virus! Why sugar coated?" asked Howard. "Any idea where this is heading?" He looked round the room searching for a reply, but everyone merely shook their heads.

"If you can use the body's own sugar system to successfully cote a virus, the body will find it almost impossible to detect that virus and fight against it!" replied Hamish.

"Can anyone substantiate what you have just told me?" asked Howard.

"Hamish, how did you end up here?" asked Linda.

"When Dusty contacted me and mentioned Prodi, I was half hoping you'd uncovered something. Let's just say that curiosity got the better of me."

"What about the New York Times, the paper you were working for? Didn't they question the events?" asked Howard, again putting out the cigar.

"At first, yes then late one morning on the third day, after Cathryn's funeral, I received word from my editor to forget the article, bury the story. I felt let down for a couple of days. I suppose the inexperience of youth, partially because I had lost Cathryn, but also because the power of the press was now being challenged. I didn't like the idea of people with power being in control of the truth. Then the morning I decided to confront my editor, he didn't arrive. He was tragically killed. His light plane exploded on take-off from his ranch, just outside New York. The FBI investigated and concluded that death was accidental, due to engine failure. His best friend, who was also his mechanic, assured me that there was nothing wrong with the engine and suspected foul play. I asked Allan if he would sign an affidavit as to how the plane was completely airworthy at the time of the accident. He was run down and killed by a hit-and-run driver while jogging that same night."

"And you think these are the same people we're involved with?" asked Bill.

At first Hamish didn't answer, and then he said, "J. Edgar died in office in '72 but his legacies and a handful of his people are still out there. I would give anything to see them finally brought to justice. My radio station, network 2W-KWB, will cover all costs and expenses."

"That's very generous of you. But why?" asked Howard, almost smiling.

"I'm still trying to piece together what became of my brother James and I suspect you people can be of help. Also, half rights to any story you uncover and most of all, to get even with Prodi for the death of Cathryn."

"You were in love with her, weren't you?" asked Linda quietly, tears forming silently in the corners of her eyes.

"Yes. We were engaged to be married that fall. But that was a long time ago," replied Hamish, the memories of his lost love flooding back to him.

"Deal," said Howard, relieving the stress that had quietly crept over the moment as the wind outside returned, lashing the willow branches forcefully against the back of the cabin and the rain outside increasing.

"Earlier, Mick," said Howard, "you mentioned something about someone's secret. Is that someone Hoover?"

Mick sighed while looking at Linda, with Bill in the background slowly nodding approval.

"I did a lot of research into the virus in Haiti, and you must remember the virus has been recorded for hundreds of years. I found a certain strain of the virus was carried by a specific species of baboon, a form of AIDS, similar to our human strain. The virus only ever affects the males. The females are for some reason, completely immune."

"I don't like where this is heading," said Howard.

"Afraid of the truth?" replied Mick, holding everyone captivated.

"On the contrary," replied Howard, embarrassed at his earlier outburst.

"Can this virus infect humans?" asked Hamish, topping up his glass yet again.

"No!" replied Mick. "But let's suppose someone in that era tampered and possibly changed the virus. The monkey virus of Haiti and the human strain are identical except for one extra human chromosome."

"What are you getting at?" asked Howard.

"Bill placed some letters on your desk last week that were sent by an anonymous doctor. In the letters he claims to have isolated a human chromosome in the monkey virus, but won't elaborate how it got there," answered Mick.

"How can that be?" asked Howard.

"I don't know. But I know that the human cell nucleus has 22 pairs and the apes 23," said Mick, having captured everyone's attention.

"What are we talking about, pairs of what?" asked Howard.

"They are the rod-like structures which occur in pairs in the cell nucleus of animals and plants and hence in every developed cell. They carry the genes, the hereditary factors and their number is constant for each species," replied Mick.

"Go on," said Howard.

"Let's suppose and it's all hypothetical at this stage that some sick person back in '69 somehow managed to change the course of history by changing a harmless monkey virus into the deadly strain of HIV that exists today. They coated the virus with the body's own sugar system then released it upon an unsuspecting homosexual sector believing the female to be immune. Never has anything so suddenly appeared anywhere on the planet with such devastating consequences, as AIDS!"

"Are you saying that these lunatics turned a monkey virus into a human virus?" asked Howard.

"Interesting scenario, don't you think?" replied Mick. "But nothing makes sense without the code, or Carlos. Actually we need both."

"Then what Cathryn was trying to tell me could tie the whole thing together!" said Hamish feeling that at long last he had come to a positive conclusion and closure about her death.

"Christ," sighed Howard.

"Christ is that all you can say? I hand you the biggest story of your life and you are so moved you reply, 'Christ,'" snorted Mick returning the cynicism he had earlier received from Howard.

"If your theory is right and I have my reservations, the people responsible can't afford any loose ends," replied Howard.

"What do you mean, loose ends?" asked Linda feeling tired and partly haggard for the evening was fast becoming late.

"Meaning whoever they are, they suspect you have stumbled onto their secret. And if what Mick believes is true, we are all in serious danger," said Hamish.

"How serious?" Mick asked.

"If we don't break the code soon and they move against us. I'd hate to think of the consequences," replied Hamish.

"Consequences?" asked Mick.

"Exactly what I'm saying. They were killers back then. They haven't changed but now the stakes have gotten bigger!" exclaimed Hamish.

"What are you saying? Again, in plain English!" asked Howard.

"The Holocaust thanks to Hitler killed seven million people. Look what the aids virus has already done to the planet. The death toll constantly mounting the expectation that millions upon millions of humans in the future are yet to die. These people are desperate and will stop at nothing. And I mean *Nothing!*" replied Hamish with force.

"Hamish is right, we need to move quickly and find out where these assholes are hiding," said Dusty with a hint of authority in his voice.

"What about the cops?" said Linda.

"What do we tell them? What do we have apart from some cryptic computer print-out and a few suspicions?" replied Mick as the door slowly creaked open and into the room stepped Saara and Nathan. The wind had all but abated with the rolling mist on the ground tumbling gently through the open door.

"Everything all right outside?" asked Dusty, placing a blanket around Saara's bare shoulders.

"Yes. All's fine," replied Nathan, in his quiet, unassuming voice.

"Is there anything I can do to help break this code?" asked Howard.

"No! But I'll keep persevering," said Mick. "With a bit of luck I might get lucky! Isn't it ironic? When the De Vinci code first surfaced, I broke it in a matter of hours. But this one's a doosy."

"Could I see those?" asked Nathan, picking up one of the pages, closely eyeing the script as he turned to Saara, her hair blown wild by the wind.

"These are the writings of the ancient ones!"

"Can you read this?" asked Mick hopefully.

"No. But I think my great-great grandfather could."

"Your great grandfather? How can he be contacted?" asked Mick excitedly.

"He lives with my mother's people, the Apache, in Arizona."

"Can he be reached? It's very important," said Linda.

"Miss Linda, he's of the Old World, a world of human beings!"

"I don't understand," she replied, neither did anyone else in the cabin. The wind once again lashed the branches of the willow tree planted by the back door, hard against the cabin walls.

"The legend is that a tribe of Navahos was once called the human beings by the other Indian nations. These people were entrusted with nurturing and guarding the Earth from all that was evil. They were the holders of everything that was good."

"What has this to do with your grandfather?" asked Howard, confusion in his face.

"My great-great-grandfather was part of that tribe when the white man came and almost overnight, decided to eradicate the red man and steal his land. Only he as a young buck survived the slaughter."

"What has this to do with reading the pages?" asked Linda.

"The writings I believe are those of the ancient Anasazi Indians, closely related to the mighty Navaho nations. Grandfather, because of the slaughter of his people does not like or respect the white ways. Even if I could contact him, I don't think he'd come."

"Nathan this is serious! He must come," replied Linda with a note of urgency in her voice.

"I'll try, Miss Linda. But I make no promises," he replied, calmly.

By now everyone had had enough. The night so quickly had slipped away and during their revelations had become disturbingly late. They could continue in the morning where they had left off tonight, if there were still issues to discuss.

Dusty moved outside with Nathan as Howard and Hamish placed themselves before the open fire, sharing a bottle of Irish malt whisky as they continued the small talk, solving the world's problems, perhaps adding a few of their own. Mick, a can of beer in hand fell to the comfort of the old leather sofa, with Linda heading for the comfort of the bedroom by the kitchen and Bill grabbing the single bed in the spare room.

Chapter 17

Bill woke early to the smell of freshly caught fish sizzling vigorously in the pan. Looking with tired eyes through the half-open door, he could see Mick still fast asleep, clutching the empty can firmly in hand. Howard along with Hamish, oblivious to the morning noises was still crashed out in their respective rocking chairs by the fireplace, long since cold and the empty whisky bottle on the floor between them. Saara was busy preparing breakfast, fish caught using the bow very effectively taught to her by Nathan.

The wind that had lashed so vigorously against the back wall of the cabin the night before had dissipated. The sun hung high in the morning sky and the lake was as smooth as glass glistening a pale blue and green to whatever creature cared to look. The wild deer had made their way along the rolling hills down to the edge of the lake, drinking and grazing along with the buffalo that inhabited the area. Ever since the magazine had purchased the valley from original land owners, the Sioux Indians, the valley and all the surrounding hills had been declared a National Park, fully protected by the American dream.

* * *

They planned for Dusty and the young ones to attempt the rescue of Carlos from the hospital, if he were still alive.

Linda and Bill were to fly to Puerto Prince, Haiti and hopefully contact Peta Maria Santos, Carlos' younger sister, in the hope she could shed some light as to how her brother had appeared after all these years, infected with AIDS and now a hunted man. Mick was to keep extracting any information he could from the Central Computer, hopefully without detection before whoever realized there was a hidden level and they started deleting the information. Howard and Hamish were to become the central contacts and if anything went wrong, station 2W-KWB at the conclusion of the weather forecast then would conclude with, 'All is not well,' informing the others that someone was in trouble.

* * *

They landed mid-morning in San Juan, Puerto Prince, the temperature in the high nineties with the humidity an intolerable ninety five percent. The airport not being air-conditioned made things unpleasant, with hundreds of confused travellers mingling in the confined area, moving in opposite directions. Loudspeakers situated around the arrival lounge blared out landing times of incoming flights and it came as a huge relief when the speakers finally fell silent. The line for a taxi stretched for a hundred metres and with tempers beginning to fray, arguments in different languages started breaking out along the queue.

Waiting patiently in line, his coat long since removed and the perspiration soaking through his shirt, Bill was visibly annoyed that the city had only a handful of cabs. The temperature that morning in San Francisco as they departed had been a low five degrees Celsius and they had both dressed accordingly. The problem now was that Linda never wore any underwear, so she couldn't publicly discard the thick sweater she was wearing.

"Bill, I can't stand the heat another minute," she cried, when a young high-pitched voice rang out from below.

"Senor, Senorita! You wish for a cab?"

Looking down, Bill observed a diminutive figure grabbing at their luggage, struggling to lift both bags.

"Yes, we are, son," replied Bill, surprised at the skinny young boy's tenacity.

"Then come with me, Senor. My uncle he owns a cab and I'm his partner," replied the small boy in his half-broken English.

"What do you think, Linda?" said Bill cautiously, half not trusting what the young lad was saying, as they had waited an eternity in the line and Bill didn't want to return to the back of the queue.

"Oh yes! I'm sick of this oppressive heat," she replied, sweat beads rolling down her face.

"OK son! Lead the way, but I'll carry these," said Bill, picking up the heavy bags, he and Linda following the young boy around the corner to the awaiting vehicle.

"You're kidding!" said Bill, half-smiling as he caught sight of the cab. "Vintage!"

Before them, parked badly across the road, was an early model 1949 Dodge, a rusted wreck with the back doors removed, eliminating the need for air-conditioning.

"Are you game, Linda? I mean, it doesn't even have seat belts."

"If I don't get out of this heat soon. It won't be a car crash that kills me. And it's a damn sight cooler than that airport," she replied, her expectations of youth showing clearly in her smile as the sweat rolled down her face.

Driving slowly across town, they arrived at the hotel that Linda had booked earlier. Its rustic charm and largely manicured gardens overlooked the city and barely visible in the distance was the ocean.

The balcony attached to their room promised space and elegance in the true Caribbean tradition. Hand painted tiles spontaneously placed around the walls blended uniquely with the milky whitewash of the hotel.

Changing into more appropriate apparel, they set off to see the sights of this delightful old city.

Their newly trustworthy guide showed them the poorer parts of the Caribbean. The streets were narrow and dirty with garbage piling up and rotting outside each dwelling. The stench in the air was almost unbearable, making it nearly impossible to travel around in a completely open vehicle. The temperature by now had soared well past the century as Linda cried out, "Pedro! Get us out of here, and make it quick!"

The smell was tearing the air from her lungs.

"Si Senora!" he replied quickly informing his uncle the driver of her wishes.

Within minutes they passed Dela Rosa Square, the place where Peta Maria owned and ran a small antique shop. The area was in total contrast to that they had earlier passed through. One could clearly define the massive class difference existing throughout the city. The streets here were wide, with the buildings lining the area painted and decorated almost in a carnival atmosphere.

They drove slowly past Peta's antique shop. A sign in the window said *'Gone for the afternoon.'* In the Caribbean it's not unusual for shops to close during the middle of the day, and then reopen later in the cool of the evening. The sun had sunk low on the horizon but still radiated the searing and relentless heat of day. Most of the other shops were also closed and the streets now almost deserted. The music drifting calmly from the local cantina sounded most inviting to Bill, however, Linda needed desperately to return to the hotel and the reassuring comfort of air-conditioning.

Linda, thanking the young boy for his service and asking him to return tomorrow, headed for the invigorating cool of the shower and the security of cold running water fresh upon her face, replacing the salty burning of perspiration put there by the excessive heat of the day.

* * *

Changed and refreshed, they sat silently on the balcony together, admiring the view, looking out over the wide expanse, sipping champagne, with the lights of the city slowly springing to life as nightfall approached. The music from the different cantinas signalled the beginning of a party usually lasting all night and well into the early hours of the next day.

The evening had visibly cooled, for Linda wearing a scant pink top showed signs of goose bumps and firming of the nipples, although the walls still pulsated with the heat of the day. The light of the full moon captivated their romantic moment.

"Will you marry me?" asked Bill quietly, a spontaneous question asked out of the blue catching Linda completely by surprise.

"What brought this on?" she said, answering his question with a question.

"We're best friends and we make a damn good team. We have great sex. Oh I almost forgot. I love you!" he answered in a soft tone as he turned up on one elbow and looking her straight in the eye.

"I have loved you for years and yes I do miss you whenever we are apart!" she answered reaching her arm out to draw him nearer.

They stared at each other's eyes for an eternity then their lips gently came together and with eyes closed they kissed and fondled each other as their bodies ravished with lust slowly came together. His hands explored every facet of her naked body carefully caressing her inner thighs as she squirmed in ecstasy. Returning his favours her hands delicately found their way across his entire body stopping at the groin with her tongue wrapping around his she gently rolled on top parting her legs as he moved to her rhythm. They made love and then made love again and again.

"I'm spent! whispered Bill while looking deep into her pale blue eyes. "I love you!" he said with perspiration rolling from his brow.

"Ditto!" replied Linda as she kissed away the sweat and holding him ever closer.

They lay on the floor talking small talk long into the night, only the stars listening to their conversation and the music of the night gently caressing their ears.

Chapter 18

Back in San Francisco, Dusty and the young ones planned the rescue of Carlos, to carefully try the impossible, to slip him from beneath the authorities' noses without anyone getting hurt, or even realize he was gone until too late. That is, if he was still alive.

Dusty, together with Nathan entered the hospital through the main doors, past reception and cautiously made their way to maternity Ward Six. Visiting hours had only just begun, so nobody paid any attention to them as they moved freely along the corridor, the flowers in Nathan's hand completing the masquerade.

The lift and stairs to the next level were heavily guarded, but shouldn't present a problem. According to Karen, Carlos remained on this level but a few yards away. Turning left into the adjoining corridor, they entered the janitor's office, locking the door behind them. Dusty, taking little time, moved Nathan up through the manhole into the fresh air duct, from here all was up to him.

Crawling rapidly on his stomach and negating each bend, Nathan reached Ward Nine. Sliding back the cover, he could hear and smell the quiet oppressive silence of pain escaping from the darkened room beneath. Slipping on the night glasses Dusty had given him earlier, Nathan moved swiftly to the floor below. His heart now pounding as the blood surged through his veins, the voices outside the door were coming ever closer, speaking in an unfamiliar language. The light flickering beneath the door was barely visible to the naked eye, but turned night into day by the use of the glasses. He counted six beds but only two were occupied, and the moaning of despair did nothing for his disposition. Nathan as a young buck had been taught by the elders, always respect life, and where ever possible, to protect the weak and utmost of all, value a life. Not the putrefaction of the flesh he witnessed before him.

Looking around, he could see the darkened room, absolutely unbearable, the stench of rotting carcasses of dead rodents lingered thick in the air and with the temperature well past the century, convinced Nathan that this place was the Devil's waiting room for grief. He controlled his pounding heart through deep breathing, the quality of the air almost turning his stomach as he located Carlos with the voices from beyond coming ever nearer. Carlos, by the wall, looked too weak to move, but having only minutes to complete his mission, risks had to be taken. Placing the frail body carefully over his shoulder, Nathan heard muffled sounds from the bed opposite.

Turning to look, a voice distinctly cried out, "Please help her! She's a friend."

The sound had come from Carlos dangling helplessly over Nathan's shoulder. Pushing Carlos up into the duct, he immediately returned to the bed behind the door, sweat now thick on his forehead. He released the restraints from the wrists then removed the gag bound firmly around the mouth. It was a female, and she slowly sat up, pulling the drip from her arm, her eyes following closely Nathan's every move.

"Can you stand?" he asked quietly, as the voices outside the room stopped, a key entered the lock.

"Yes! I think so," she replied in barely a whisper as Nathan quickly moved her gently against the wall, the door to the room half opening. His heart began racing when he reached for his knife with his right hand, the left he held firmly against his chest trying to quieten the noise coming from within. The light when the door opened partially blinded Nathan with the pain cutting deep into his brain, but somehow he kept his silence, the door once more slammed shut as the footsteps vanished quickly into the distance.

"Please lead me to the duct," he pleaded, removing the glasses but the light still burning deep in his eyes.

"What's wrong?" she whispered.

"Nothing, Please do as I ask," he replied, for he knew time was fast running out. He made his way into the roof and pulled her up behind him, then placing Carlos over his shoulder, they quickly clawed their way back to Dusty. An eternity had passed by the time he slid Carlos into the safety of the big man's arms. The woman followed closely as Nathan replaced the cover, leaving no signs as to how they had snatched the couple from beneath their noses. The woman had improved rapidly since being removed from the drip, the colour in her cheeks slowly returning.

"Thanks," she said as Dusty gently lifted her upon the table, for she still showed signs of drowsiness, her knees slightly buckling beneath her.

"Are you all right?" she said looking at Nathan with concern.

"Everything's fine," he replied for the blindness had only been temporary.

"Let's get out of here. By my calculations, the janitor's due back any minute," said Dusty, placing Carlos in the wheel chair which had been left earlier by some previous patient. Using the service elevator, avoiding any attention, they made their way from the hospital to the car park where Saara waited patiently. Dusty thought that the operation had gone well, almost too well. Why the guards to the next level? Who the hell was so important that they needed security? Especially in a hospital and above all, why US Naval MPs?

"Where to?" asked Saara, snapping Dusty back to reality.

"To the Weekly," he replied, keeping one eye on the mirror, watching to see that no one followed.

Now to vanish, keep Carlos out of sight, but the problem was to where? Even though nothing had happened so far, the feeling was always there, something was about to happen and Dusty didn't want to get caught out.

Chapter 19

Puerto Prince, the following morning was heavily overcast, keeping the temperature respectable. Linda, already dressed, moved to the balcony with Bill joining her a short time later for breakfast. Pedro had arrived earlier; in fact he'd been there since dawn, waiting patiently for them to awaken. And being their personal guide, he felt it safe to help himself to the food on offer whilst quaintly chatting in his broken English.

"Senor Bill! Telephone in the foyer," said the young waitress, discreetly making her way to their private table.

"Thank you," replied Bill as she disappeared back to the kitchen. It was Howard, informing Bill things had gone well, however they had one concern about Sister Karen and weren't sure if she could be trusted. Bill assured him she could, and all going well they would be home by the weekend.

Driving leisurely through the narrow streets stopping occasionally to browse at the open markets scattered throughout the back lanes, they entered Dela Rosa Square stopping opposite Peta's old-fashioned antique shop. Pedro remained outside on the mats provided, assuming a siesta position beneath his large sombrero, bought earlier through Linda's generosity. Inside, a tall, drop-dead gorgeous, slim lady warmly greeted them. Her dark complexion and silky long black hair, tiny waist with wide hips the firmest stomach accentuated her perfect hourglass figure.

"Hi! I'm Peta," she said, extending her hand in friendship.

"Delighted to meet you," replied Linda. "I'm Linda and this is my man, Bill," making Bill feel like a dog on a leash. Browsing through the antiques, he couldn't help notice the girls had somehow instantaneously become best friends. He'd earlier put a smile on Peta's face as he couldn't remove his eyes from her sensual hips and she caught his glance when turning to answer the phone. The sun outside had once again returned, with Pedro moving inside to avoid the sweltering heat.

Time passed quickly and it was now time to leave; Peta with previous obligations would be closing for the afternoon and Bill felt he could use a cool refresher, a San Miguel, the local beer.

"Bill," said Linda. "Peta has asked us to join her for dinner at her favourite haunt, Garcia's Café."

"Bill!" said Peta. "Linda told me about the chillies you wrestled with last night. I assure you this is different."

The chillies Bill had dined on the previous night had all but set him on fire, his stomach still asking the questions. But they had come searching for answers, and what better place to ask the questions than during dinner surrounded by beautiful people?

"Why not?" replied Bill, helping Pedro to his feet and moving slowly outside to the awaiting wreck of a cab.

* * *

That evening, arriving at the tavern early, Bill along with Linda savoured the delightful atmosphere of this unique Latin American bar. One could smell the different aromas of Cuban cigars drifting gently across the darkened, smoke-filled room. Peta, elegantly dressed, entered the tavern through the kitchen to the vibrant sounds of a Mexican quartet playing the Macarena, the local dance phenomenon that had swept the country years earlier.

"What a unique place," said Linda as she greeted Peta with a kiss and a smile and Bill standing to acknowledge her presence. The main room of the cantina was rocking to the sound of loud vibrant Mexican music. "Been coming here long?" she asked, sipping from a long cool glass.

"Since my brother mysteriously disappeared, Garcia's been like family," replied Peta, as a waitress escorted them to a private booth.

They dined and danced well into the night with the small talk slowly turning to Carlos.

"What's this about?" asked Peta. "Who are you people?" her tone becoming wary as it seemed they were avoiding the questions she was asking.

"We're friends," replied Bill, observing the softness of her skin and feeling her dilemma for the questions she was being asked.

"Are you agents? Are you FBI?" asked Peta, looking to the bar for help.

"No! On the contrary, we're reporters," answered Linda, now anxious to calm the situation as she too felt the tension between them steadily growing.

"Why do you need to know about Carlos?" A puzzled look crept onto Peta's face.

"We're extremely interested in the people he worked with," replied Bill, wanting to tell her everything but not sure about how to break the news of Carlos having AIDS and worse, perhaps with only weeks to live.

"Do you have any photos of your brother?" asked Linda reaching out for Peta's hand.

"You did not answer my question!" replied Peta. "And no, I don't possess any photos of Carlos!" She stood up, ready to leave, the look in her eyes one of terror.

"Please, Peta, sit down. Your brother's alive. He's with friends back home," said Bill hurriedly, seeing the frightened look.

"Exactly where is back home?" asked Peta.

"San Francisco," said Linda. "But he's very ill." Her eyes were firmly fixed on two huge Haitians making their way towards them.

"Why, what's wrong?" Peta asked, her voice partially drowned by the music and the noises emanating from the bar.

"Carlos.." Linda paused, looking to Bill and holding Peta's hand ever so gently. "Your brother has AIDS and possible only weeks to live," she continued, looking caringly into Peta's eyes, a nervous smile appearing on her lips.

"AIDS? Carlos could not have AIDS, he isn't a homosexual," replied Peta, tears of emotion slowly forming in her eyes for such had been their closeness ever since childhood.

"You don't have to be homosexual to contract AIDS," replied Bill carefully, the compassion in his voice reflecting the thoughts of their explanation.

"I don't understand," replied Peta in her soft tone. "How could my brother have contracted AIDS if he wasn't homosexual?"

"That's a whole new story and we really don't have the time to quibble!" answered Bill bluntly. "Peta I'm sorry to be so abrupt. And my questions may seem callous, but our time is fast running out."

"Peta, did Carlos say anything unusual before he vanished?" asked Linda, her eyes now firmly fixed on Peta's.

"No! He took nothing and said even less," Peta replied waving away the two huge Haitian bouncers. "Why?"

"I'm not sure! I was hoping perhaps you had some answers," replied Bill, his voice echoing loudly around the room as the band had stopped playing.

"He did however ask me to mind a small metal box. And to trust no one," she whispered, as every eye in the room seemed to be looking towards their table as the music started once again.

"Could we see it?" asked Linda, again sipping from her glass.

"On one condition," Peta replied.

"And what condition would that be?" asked Linda.

"That I accompany you back to San Francisco. It's imperative I talk to Carlos. If only for the last time!"

Bill shuddered at the thought of involving this beautiful innocent woman in their affairs, but he needed desperately to look inside the box, believing it could possibly hold the key to the code.

* * *

Leaving the tavern late that evening, a calm night greeted the trio. The stars scattered around the heavens brightly glistened, flickering light towards anyone who cared to look. The air turned cool and with the lateness of the evening the atmosphere became refreshing and clean, a far cry from the earlier steamy humidity endured during the day. Walking slowly along the narrow lanes exchanging ideas as to how Carlos had vanished years earlier, the friendship and bond between them grew. Trust replaced suspicion, with Peta finally asking the question that had tormented her all night.

"Why are you and Linda really in Haiti? And what has this to do with my brother?"

"Peta, that's complicated! I'll do my best to answer your question," replied Bill, gently placing an arm around each woman's waist as they walked leisurely out beneath the star-filled sky.

"Linda and I, with help from friends are researching the story of AIDS. The compassionate side, a story for so long suppressed through ignorance and untruths. Hopefully we can change the way people feel towards the stricken," continued Bill as they rounded the last corner leading to Peta's shop.

Suddenly a black limousine burst out of the blackness, the windows heavily tinted and almost collecting Linda as the vehicle sped past.

"That's Victor's car!" yelled Peta, her eyes closely following the dust as the vehicle hurriedly raced away. "Why would he try to run us down?" she said, looking into Linda's confused eyes, her heart pounding for the nearness of death had frightened her very existence. "He's a friend," she concluded.

"No one was trying to run anyone down. I think we were being served a warning," replied Bill, himself upset at the closeness of the vehicle.

"A warning about what?" replied Peta, still visibly upset as she held Linda tightly by the hand.

"I'm not sure. But the answer I think lies in there," replied Bill as they approached her premises. They stopped halfway across the road in amazement to view the damage caused to the shop. The front doors had been violently ripped from their hinges and artefacts from within were scattered throughout the walkway and half way across the road.

"Why?" asked Peta. "Nothing like this has ever happened to me before. Why would anyone in their right mind want to destroy an antique shop?" She stared at the damage to the premises, shaking her head in disbelief.

"Who knows what valuables your shop contains?" said Linda trying to console Peta.

"It wasn't robbery, although it's made out to look like that," replied Bill.

"They're after the box and I don't think anything will stop them," said Bill, as Peta and Linda moved slowly and carefully across the shattered pieces towards the rear of the premises. At the same time a police vehicle pulled up outside, with two large uniformed men entering.

"Peta!" yelled Bill, as his Spanish was non-existent and these guys looked like they meant business.

The two men talked briefly to Peta and left as suddenly as they had arrived with Bill not sure what Peta had said, but he felt huge relief when the car slowly moved off.

"Did you call the police?" asked Bill, with Peta again making her way to the rear of the shop.

"No," she replied, turning and pointing to a large hole in the wall, once the phone but now only a few coloured wires dangling loosely from the cavity.

"Any luck?" asked Bill as dawn slowly appeared.

"Shit!" came the reply from the back. "There's so much damage. The assholes have virtually destroyed everything."

"We could use some help back here," yelled Linda. Bill, reluctant earlier, knew then that Peta had to go with them. Her innocence would be no defence against whoever was trying to warn them off. And surely it would only be a matter of time before her name became a statistic in some small, unsolved police file.

Eventually, with painstaking patience, Peta located the small metal box, but the lid over the years, had rusted firmly shut.

"Let's get away from here!" said Bill, suspecting the uniformed men were not the police, but someone sent to check them out.

"Are you not interested in what's inside?" inquired Peta, carefully removing some broken glass from a beautifully handcrafted tapestry swinging aimlessly from the western wall.

"I am! But let's look elsewhere," he replied, gesturing to Linda to hurry.

Chapter 20

Returning to the imagined safety of the hotel and over an early morning coffee they decided that Peta would be safer staying with them, returning to her apartment later in the day when there were people present and moving around.

Midday had come and gone as they approached her unit, again the black limousine sped off and it came as no surprise to find the front door forced open with the apartment partially destroyed.

"My god! Is that metal box so important that it can cause this?" asked Peta. The word 'eliminate' had been written on the bedroom mirror in a thick, almost black lipstick. Neither answered, but Linda quickly helped Peta pack, taking only the essentials necessary for a woman's survival. Meanwhile Bill rang the airport to book the first available flight to San Francisco. No flights to the States direct were available. There was, however, flight 611 to Mexico departing at four, with a connecting flight to San Francisco later that evening. Time had grown short for it was well past two, and with the flight departing within hours, they now had to hurry.

Back at their hotel they discovered Pedro, exceedingly distressed, squatting, waiting for their return outside the main gates.

"Senor Bill!" he cried, tears of pain in his eyes. "Policeman hurt Greico!"

"Pedro, slow down. I can't understand a word you're saying," replied Bill, helping Peta with her luggage as time was becoming extremely short.

"The police first they smash your and Miss Linda's room, then hit my friend Greico!" sobbed Pedro with Bill moving closer to console him.

Greico was the part time manager who had befriended Linda and Bill earlier in the week with the mix-up of their room booked via the Internet before leaving San Francisco.

"Pedro, are you sure they were the police?" asked Bill.

"Si Senor! Two men in police uniforms came out of a large black car with very dark windows."

Ramos, Bill thought to himself. The man had been there in person. He had become desperate and desperate men do desperate things.

Bill cautiously entered the kitchen through reception. Amongst the scattered pots and pans lay a bleeding Greico, and judging by the destruction and the damage throughout, he must have put up a gutsy fight. Linda and Peta managed to stop most of the bleeding and it wasn't long after the ambulance arrived to take him to hospital.

Bill phoned the airport from reception, hoping to arrange a later flight. However, 611 was the only available aircraft leaving Haiti until the following Tuesday. Also, any unused tickets would revert immediately to standby if their bookings weren't confirmed within the next half hour. The time now well past three, the airport at best thirty five minutes away and the fact they still had to pack, made it impossible to catch that flight.

"Bill! I have a friend in Ponce!" said Peta, learning about the flight arrangements. "Perhaps she could fly us to Mexico?"

"You have a friend with her own aircraft?"

"Yes! Leanne often flies to the States on business."

"But we still have to get to Ponce," said Linda, holding a sobbing Pedro close to her bosom.

"That's not a problem," replied Bill. "We'll simply borrow Greico's van, he won't be using it for a while."

* * *

Linda hurriedly packed for the trip with some help from Peta while Bill rang Howard back in the States, inquiring where Mr. Ramos fitted into the Carlos saga.

"What seems to be the problem?" Howard asked.

"Somehow, we've disturbed a Mr. Ramos. I'd like some background on the man if that's possible."

"I'll put Mick on," replied Howard, for he knew nothing of Ramos.

"Bill! What's the problem?" asked Mick's lively voice.

"What do we know about a Mister Ramos?" asked Bill.

"Ah, yes! Victor Ramos the right hand man to J. Edgar Hoover during the early and late sixties. But for some unknown reason he also disappeared in '87," said Mick.

"That's it?" replied Bill, hoping for a slightly more enlightening answer.

"Sorry! Each time I enter the computer, someone's deleting, removing everything. And I mean everything."

"Do you have any idea as to who?" asked Bill

"Nope but it's definitely not coming from this end. It's emanating from Washington," replied Mick.

"Washington!" said Bill. "Who the hell do we know in the capital that could want this shit erased?"

"I wish I could help you. But at the moment I can't even help myself!" answered Mick.

"Any luck with the code?" asked Bill, hoping against hope.

"Not yet! But I'm still working on it."

"What about Nathan's grandfather?"

"He can't be found. He's off somewhere in the hills cleansing his soul."

"Sorry Mick, we really have to be going," replied Bill, noticing the girls were packed and ready to leave, and also wanting to avoid any further visits from Ramos.

"A problem?" asked Mick.

"Put it this way - I suspect we've been warned."

"By Ramos?" said Mick.

"We think so! But we can't prove a thing!" replied Bill.

"Linda has another of those letters hand written and delivered to the front desk," said Mick.

"Did we finally get a look at the person delivering the letter?" asked Bill.

"No. Clare was at lunch and the young casual can't remember anyone even coming through the doors," answered Mick.

"You want to read me the letter over the phone?" asked Bill.

"No! Just be safe and I'll see you guys back here."

"Everything all right?" asked Linda, sitting beside Peta on the plush foyer lounge, for she had overheard the conversation he had had with Mick.

"Just a minor hiccup," he replied, as now would be the hardest thing for saying goodbye to Pedro and explaining why they couldn't take him along.

Chapter 21

The journey from San Juan to Ponce would last no longer than two hours for the 120 kilometre distance, but he didn't want to arrive there that night, feeling they would be safer staying somewhere between the cities. That is, if Ramos had truly become desperate and as such was still lurking in the shadows. Pedro's face lit up when Linda handed him a stack of fifty dollar notes, twelve months' wages in this part of the world, but the sadness of Greico's beating was still evident in his eyes and their departure did little to cheer him up. His father had passed away a year ago, making Pedro the main provider for his mother and three younger sisters. So remain he must.

As the van pulled away they could see the tiny figure, tears streaming down his face his lips quivering, waving his last goodbye, and all the while trying valiantly to hold a smile.

Peta drove discreetly along the back streets and lanes on the way out of the city, making sure no one followed and as the miles slowly passed the countryside turned to jungle containing all forms of elaborate wildlife. The peaceful serenity of the area was only disturbed by the noise of the van rumbling along the bumpy track, supposedly a highway.

Thirty minutes from Ponce, Peta turned off the main road down a small track unused for years, winding through the lush countryside to a clearing partially surrounded by a crystal clear blue pond. A free flowing waterfall splashing down coloured cliffs fed the minute water hole. The setting sun bathed the falling droplets along with the rising mist, displaying a brilliant kaleidoscope of colours.

"It's beautiful!" said Linda, stepping carefully from the van, words failing to adequately describe the magnificence of the hidden valley, untouched for decades

"This is the place our parents came when Carlos and I were young. We should be safe here for the night. No one knows about it but us," replied Peta, her memory casting back to happier moments in the past.

*　*　*

Night passed quickly and in the morning Bill woke to the sounds of laughter, with the sun gently splashing rays of light through the crystal clear waters and the noise of wildlife at times almost deafening.

It was easy to forget one's troubles in the beauty of the countryside. Linda was swimming and such was the clarity of the water that every facet of her naked form was completely visible. Peta under the waterfall gently caressing her body in tune with nature had the figure of a young endowed girl, although she was well past the age of fifty. Slim yet curvy with two tiny dimples in the small of her back, the breasts firm and natural were partially hidden by her long silky smooth hair flowing down a well tanned body.

When Peta waved, Bill couldn't react quickly enough, and as a result didn't notice Linda walking towards him.

"William!" The name she always used when being blunt. "You're supposed to be looking at me. Not her! Or don't you find me attractive anymore?"

"Darling, you're beautiful," he pleaded, blushing at her nakedness. Linda had the body of a goddess. Beautiful unspoiled breasts, the nipples hard and firm strutting out erect, he suspected from the cool of the pond. Her legs could be no longer, perfectly shaped from toe to hip. A tiny waist complemented her flat stomach, the buttocks firm and full. Very little pubic hair exposed the exactness of her body and one could clearly see she was a quietly confident person, a woman unto herself.

"Sorry. I couldn't help myself," he said sheepishly, like a child caught with his hand in the cookie jar.

"I was being a bitch. You men are all the same," came her reply with a smile on her lips. "You can't help yourselves," she said teasingly drying her slender legs. "You're right, she is attractive. But you only look."

"Darling, you know me!"

"Yeah and that's a worry!" replied Linda in a half smiling tone.

"And besides, you're enough woman for any man," said Bill as Peta slowly walked back, her hips gently swaying with each step taken. She too had very little hair and the smile on her face said it all. When she reached for the towel the bulge in Bill's jeans became quite pronounced, with both girls bursting into laughter.

"Going for a swim, Bill?" Linda asked, patting herself dry, with the sun glistening brightly off the shimmering pale blue water.

"I don't think so," he replied, trying in vain to hide his embarrassment. "It's difficult for a man not to get aroused and even harder not to show his intentions when you have two attractive females, flaunting their naked bodies. But I'm not complaining."

"What male would?" said Linda with a smile.

Both girls dressed as Bill started preparing breakfast from the back of the van.

* * *

The morning moved all too quickly and leaving this place was difficult, but leave they must. As the sun rose high into the morning sky, they continued on to Ponce. The road didn't improve, but the potholes became fewer. Jungle gave way to housing as they fast approached the city.

"Anyone hungry?" asked Bill, turning down the volume of the radio, admiring the view across the mountain range, the atmosphere clean and fresh while in the distance lay a haze of smog.

"Let's stop a while," replied Peta.

"I wouldn't mind visiting the bathroom," said Linda as the van pulled up outside Ponce's equivalent to America's McDonalds.

"I'll order some refreshments while you girls powder your noses," said Bill, stretching his legs as he climbed out and moved towards the restaurant.

Seated on the outside rear veranda overlooking the hills dotted by housing, suburbia at its worst, he was again joined by Peta carrying the local paper.

"Bill! Look at this," she said, placing the paper on the table in front of him.

"What is it, Peta?" replied Bill, staring at the destruction on the front page.

"The flight we were booked on yesterday, Flight 611 to Mexico. It crashed during take-off. All two hundred and forty-three, including crew, died in the inferno that followed. There were no survivors," she said, her eyes leaving the paper and turning to Bill, his mind in turn flashing back to the story Hamish had told about the time his editor was killed in a similar supposed accident.

"Does it explain how the accident happened?" asked Bill, looking further into the paper, searching for more detailed information but bewildered by the language, while holding Peta's hand ever so gently.

"No. The authorities have no idea, but suspect sabotage, but no one's claimed responsibility!" she answered.

"And I bet no one does," said Bill, as he was now completely convinced that the accident of Flight 611 had been instigated and carried out by Ramos.

"Peta, would you mind awfully ringing your friend?"

"I've only just spoken to Leanne. She'd be delighted with the extra company across the Caribbean."

"When is she leaving for Mexico?" asked Bill, as Linda joined them.

"Have I missed something?" she asked, sitting herself next to Peta.

"Look at this," replied Bill, placing the paper in front of her.

"My God!" exclaimed Linda as Peta explained the havoc on the front page, with Bill adding his suspicions. "What's wrong with these people? Doesn't life mean anything to them? Will they stop at nothing?"

"I can't imagine what's driving them. It must be something in that computer we have innocently discovered," replied Bill looking at both girls and shaking his head. "And they most certainly don't want the contents made public."

"Oh Bill! I want to go home," Linda cried, feeling the arduous burden of bereavement. Whole families had perished in the inferno, the stupidity of these people doing as they wished with no-one to answer to.

"Darling, we are heading home," he replied, passing Linda his hankie to help dry her tear-filled eyes. "Soon as Peta's friend Leanne is ready, we're out of here."

Chapter 22

That afternoon they landed in Mexico, their luck holding. If Ramos were after them there would be no way of tracing their departure. Leanne didn't have to file a flight plan or passenger list. Ramos may even believe they perished in the earlier air disaster. Either way, Bill felt sure they had given him the slip, at least for the moment.

They exchanged thankyous and good-byes in the departure lounge of the Flight 726 bound for San Francisco. Leanne, her figure short but curvy and with a wicked sense of humour had known Peta the past fourteen years, their friendship never questioned. The girls had met the day after Carlos' disappearance and the bonding between them strengthened as time passed. Each would gladly sacrifice all for the other.

Time had slipped by all too quickly and with the final call for boarding they said their last farewells, a tear appearing in the corner of Peta's eye as she hugged her friend lovingly. Leanne too, quietly wept as they embraced each other in a way only good friends could.

* * *

The flight home was smooth and uneventful with Bill being pleasantly surprised when Linda gently shook him awake.

"Darling it's time to wake up. We've landed," she said.

"Where?" he asked, yawning as he stretched comfortably back in his seat.

"San Francisco," replied Linda, her eyes feeling extremely tired from the trip.

"That was quick," said Bill as Peta stretched her legs in the aisle, her mini slightly wrinkled from the time spent sitting.

"Quick! You slept the whole way!" smiled Linda. "I'm convinced that you could sleep on a barbed wire fence in a snowstorm."

"OK! What did you girls get up to?" he asked, observing both their smiling faces, a hint of the prankster in Linda's eyes.

"If only you knew!" Linda replied, again smiling at Peta who discreetly smiled back, a worrying sign to Bill.

He rang Howard when they had finally cleared customs letting him know they were back and safe.

"Come over and bring the girls," said Howard.

"Howard, it's past midnight! We're dog tired."

"Mick's here with me, please!" replied Howard, triggering Bill's curiosity.

"Howard wants us at the office!" said Bill to the tired looking girls waiting patiently with their luggage as he clicked off the phone.

"What! Now?" replied Linda. "I was really looking forward to some bed time and much needed sleep."

"Mick's with your dad!" replied Bill.

"What's so important it can't wait until morning?" she said, shaking her head at Peta.

"Didn't say," replied Bill, placing an arm around each girl and moving outside to a waiting cab.

* * *

Arriving at the magazine, they were intercepted by two security guards.

"Dad's never had people on the door!" exclaimed Linda, horrified and astonished by the presence of the guards.

"He has now," replied Bill as they were quietly escorted from the foyer by Jo Anne, Howard's personal secretary.

"Jo, are you still here?" said Linda, not meaning it the way it sounded.

"More and more these days!" Jo replied politely. "There's so much to do and so little time to do it in!"

She led them out of the elevator, entering Howard's office. Mick was seated in one of the plush leather lounges, a newspaper in one hand and a cold cup of coffee in the other.

"People! I'd like to introduce our friend Peta!" said Linda with Mick standing to acknowledge their entrance.

"You must excuse the way I look. We have been travelling all day, since first light!" said Peta.

"Don't apologize! You look fine," replied Jo.

"If you'd care to freshen up please feel free!" Jo said, pointing the way to Howard's personal en-suite.

"Gracias," she replied, closing the door quietly behind her.

"Jo! I know it's late, but could you possibly hustle some coffee for our guests?" asked Howard entered the office through the study.

"I'll try sir!" she replied, with Peta re-entering the room.

"Dad this is our friend Peta! She's Carlos's younger sister."

"Pleasure!" replied Howard, a slight tremor in his voice, shaking her hand gently.

"Howard! Why the guards?" asked Bill as Jo returned carrying a tray of cups and a large pot of coffee.

"Bill, in the past few days, yours and Mick's apartment has been completely demolished."

"Not again!" Bill yawned looking over to Mick, sitting shaking his head in response to Howard's statement.

"This time for keeps, the whole building has been levelled."

"Anyone hurt?" asked Bill.

"Luckily the old building that you two live in was empty at the time," answered Howard. "But even if it wasn't, I don't think that would have deterred them!"

"Are we sure who we're dealing with?" said Bill.

"I'll get to that!" replied Howard. "Dusty's avoided two sniper attempts and the death threats appear daily on the Internet. The mail on the net is the same each morning. The word 'eliminate' appears in black. If we don't return Carlos to the hospital and forget this story, we will be in no uncertain terms, 'Eliminated!'"

"Howard! There has to be some way we can stop whoever these people are!" said Bill. "I mean stopping short of murder!"

"The way it's going, killing may be an option!" said Howard.

"Victor Ramos! As Mick told you over the phone, he has resurfaced. But the FBI has no knowledge of him after 1987. It's as though he just ceased to exist!" said Howard.

"He's resurfaced all right! With a vengeance," replied Bill, his mind casting back to the Haitian disaster. "And I suspect he's responsible for the crash of Flight 611."

"I'll get someone down there to check it out," replied Howard.

"Now Victoria Prodi she has also re-entered the picture. She seems every bit as ruthless as Mr. Ramos but a lot harder to track down," said Mick.

"How so?" asked Bill with Linda and Peta now quietly asleep in their respective leather lounges.

"I'm not sure," replied Mick. "Each time I enter the computer, the level containing the Messiah was being deleted. I assume these people stumbled on to the same program that took me an accident to find!"

"Suppose they helped co-write the level. Wouldn't that answer some questions?" asked Bill, placing a blanket around each of the girls.

"Certainly, but I'm of the opinion that Carlos wrote the entire level without their knowledge, replied Mick. "He's somehow warning us about these fanatics. How they will stop at nothing. Also some atrocious act committed in the late sixties. Something so vile they're willing to kill to protect themselves."

"How can you be so sure?" asked Howard, lighting up his cigar.

"I'm not! But nothing else makes sense!" said Mick. "Carlos had to have operated on his own. And how he entered his message undetected into the computer defies all logic. Unless I crack the code, we will never know for certain." He yawned loudly.

"Where are Dusty, Nathan and Saara?" asked Linda, waking slowly from her short slumber.

"The three of them moved Carlos to the Apache reservation in Arizona!" replied Howard with his head resting comfortably in his left palm.

"The Apache reservation in Arizona?" asked Linda with a confused look on her tired face. "Why the Apache reservation?"

"To gain access to the reservation you have to be blood related or be accompanied by blood to enter!" explained Mick, again yawning vigorously.

"How is my brother?" asked Peta, gently wiping the sleep from her tired eyes.

"We don't know. They haven't been heard from for days. But I'm sure he's fine!" said Howard, sipping from his cup while still puffing heavily on the cigar.

"Thank you!" Peta replied.

"Any luck at all with the coded pages?" said Bill.

"Not yet. Not until we contact Nathan's grandfather," replied Mick, himself by now half asleep.

"And when might that be?" asked Linda, standing to stretch.

"Darling, the best people are out searching. But he's vanished into the Valley of Ten Thousand Smokes. If he doesn't want to be found, he won't be!" replied Howard.

"What is the Valley of Ten Thousand Smokes?" asked Peta.

"They're geysers somewhere in the Grand Canyon," said Howard

"If he can't be found or won't be found, how the hell is Mick going to unravel the code?" asked Linda. "I mean the Grand Canyon. That's a big place. Where do you start?"

"Don't look at me," said Mick. "I've run out of ideas. Without the old Indian I don't have an answer."

"There must be a simple solution. Something we've overlooked" replied Linda half hoping to rekindle Mick's intense curiosity.

"If we have, I can't see it. And there's nothing left in the computer!" replied Mick starting to get annoyed with Linda's assumption that more could be done to crack the code.

"Ok then, where do we go from here?" asked Howard.

"The second letter! Where is it? asked Linda, looking directly at Howard.

"Right here," replied Howard opening the draw and searching for the letter with tired hands. When he finally located the letter he handed it directly to Linda.

"Are you going to open it or just sit there and stare at it?" he asked sarcastically.

"I'm sorry!" replied Linda. "Look at the hand writing," she said as she tore open the envelope.

"What do you mean?" asked Mick thinking that he had missed something.

"The scribbled hand writing! What does that suggest?" she replied.

"I don't understand!" said Mick looking at Bill to see if he could shed some light on the matter.

"The last time I saw hand writing like this was when I was interviewing students in year two," came Linda's reply.

"Do you think that these letters are coming from a minor? And if so! Who?" asked Bill again yawning as the night started turning into day through the window.

"No I don't! But whoever is sending us these letters is either unable to write on his own for whatever reason, or he can't speak the language and has a young friend helping with the lingo."

"What's it say?" asked Mick, wanting the night to end.

"Sorry!" replied Linda as she started to read the letter aloud.

"This is my second contact and hopefully not my last. I applaud you for getting my friend from the hospital. There are now people associated with the White House that you must be wary of. They have much to lose and will stop at nothing. My time I feel will end shortly for they are closing in fast and there is nowhere left to hide. You now have the key to the code so use it wisely and quickly before they have the chance to silence you."

She looked up at the group. "The letter was again signed, '*a friend*'".

"What does he mean about you having the key to the code?" asked Howard.

"I don't know!" replied Linda shaking her head.

"Sir, these girls are dog tired and this is getting us nowhere. Can't we continue this conversation some other time," said Bill, himself feeling strongly the urge for sleep, although he'd slept all the way from Mexico.

"You're right. I'm sorry I insisted you come over. I'll have Jo drive you guys to your mother's."

"Why mum's?" asked Linda.

"I had Mick move everything that could be saved from your apartment after the bombing."

"Dad, these people.." began Linda.

"I know. And I promise we will get to the bottom of this," replied Howard convincing himself that what he was saying was achievable.

Chapter 23

Since returning from Haiti, the trio had taken up residence at Linda's mother's home, a huge palatial mansion very prominent in the hills overlooking San Francisco, the wealthier part of town. Swimming pools and movie stars were the norm. A complete security system installed years earlier by Dusty ensured unwanted entry became well-nigh impossible, and with Linda's mother overseas holidaying for the winter, they only had themselves to worry about. The weather remained unusually warm for this time of year, enticing the girls with their wicked sense of humour, wearing the briefest of swimwear, most days only the tiniest G-string separating them from the full Monty, to use the pool regularly.

One scorching afternoon, Bill lying innocently beside the pool reading the research they had compiled about aids while cooking the ladies lunch, was suddenly attacked from behind and dragged struggling into the refreshingly cool water of the pool. Both women in a mood to play, wearing next to nothing, wanted to give Bill a memorable afternoon to thank him for the patience he had shown over the past few days in dealing with their swinging moods and changing desires.

Linda, the natural blonde complemented the contrasting brunette of Peta, each girl sporting deep all over tans. Peta, though older, retained the figure of a woman much younger. In fact they could easily be mistaken for sisters. They talked, played and splashed until lunch was ready as Bill, always the perfect gentleman, prepared their table. A light salad served with a tantalizing French dressing, closely followed by all the exotic seafoods imaginable, topped off with a bottle of white wine, made the afternoon perfect. The sun though sinking low in the western sky gently warmed their bodies with the palms around the pool swaying gracefully in the breeze, making for an enjoyable day.

Eventually, the weather turned cool and the outside sauna became the place to relax. Bill's modesty had been tested to the absolute limit, but now vanished when he joined the women in their half naked state. Peta with tiny beads of perspiration trickling sweetly down her body was the first to break the silence.

"Bill, it's been a week! When may I meet my brother?" He felt his manhood increase but for some unknown reason, didn't feel embarrassed. He did however try to cover the moment with a hand, turning slightly to one side with both girls smiling broadly.

"Ladies you're making my situation extremely difficult."

"Why?" asked Linda, again smiling at Peta and receiving a smile in return.

"When may I see Carlos?" repeated Peta flaunting her slim frame and adjusting her G-string, higher upon her hips. "When are we finally going to meet?" she said, her hair wet from the heat and perspiration of the sauna. Tiny beads of sweat dripped delicately from her chin, and then trickled tantalizingly down her cleavage.

"I spoke to Dusty at length last night, so we'll be leaving for Arizona in the morning."

"Why didn't you tell us this earlier? What took you so long?" replied Linda standing, stretching her legs as the beads of perspiration rolled daintily from her toes. "And what's Mick up to these days?"

Why would I, thought Bill to himself. What person in their right mind would willingly give up a day like this? A day most men would kill for. A day straight from the pages of Playboy! Peta at the same time moved slowly to claim her towel from the seat opposite, her nakedness becoming too much for Bill as he closed his eyes to answer Linda's question.

"Mick is attempting to run a trace on the plates of the Ford," he said but his eyes remained firmly shut.

"And?" Linda said, wrapping her towel tightly around her body and gently folding the hair over her shoulder.

"Nothing, the car doesn't exist!"

"Another blank," she replied, thoughtfully brushing her hair.

"I'll give them one thing! They're good," said Bill, trying further to protect his modesty.

"Come-on Peta, let's go! I feel Bill becoming excited again!" smiled Linda with both girls disappearing quickly towards the main house. Left sitting quietly in the sauna he thought to himself. How the hell could a normal red blooded male not get aroused with two stunning females flaunting their wares with not a hint of modesty? After all he was only a man!

Completing a long cold shower, Bill cautiously returned to the house. The girls already dressed much to his relief were busy packing for the trip ahead with great expectation. They would be travelling light using no credit cards, only cash and in the comfort of Linda's mother's Range Rover, a rare off-road vehicle by American standards but very popular throughout Europe.

By using cash Bill knew their trail would be impossible to follow, allowing them the freedom to enjoy the trip to Arizona.

Chapter 24

Leaving early the following morning before dawn enabled them to exit San Francisco before the dreaded peak hour traffic. With no Ford in sight they felt relieved, singing along with the radio as they distanced themselves from the city. Taking turns to drive the 800 mile long haul, they kept moving across California, Nevada and into Arizona, stopping only to change drivers, refuel and buy a meal. But it wasn't until reaching the Grand Canyon late that evening that Mother Nature showed her splendour.

Standing together at the gateway, hand in hand, they looked upon the shadowy images formed by clouds shifting along the canyon walls with the might of the Colorado River at the bottom of the cliffs wildly winding her way towards the sea.

"I can now see why Nathan's great great grandfather, can't be found," said Linda holding Peta's hand and awed at the size of the Grand Canyon.

"Beautiful, isn't she?" said Bill but wanting to continue with their journey as they still had a hundred miles left to travel and the hopes of reaching the reservation before dark had gone. They finally continued with the highway ahead forming illusionary figures dancing in the distance, created by the heat rising from the road and the sudden cold of darkness. With an hour still to travel, Bill called Dusty on his mobile phone, informing him of their arrival.

As they were expected much earlier, they now would not arrive until after dark.

* * *

"We'll be there shortly," said Bill leaning forward speaking loudly into the phone mounted centrally on the dash. "We're just passing some old ruins off in the distance."

"How is Carlos?" asked Peta quietly, unable to resist the opportunity to communicate with her brother.

"Who's that?" replied Dusty, his voice crackling wildly from static over the open speaker.

"Dusty! I would like to introduce you to Peta, younger sister to Carlos!" answered Bill, a smile on his face.

"I look forward to meeting you Peta. And yes, he's resting comfortably. A few unexpected turns but Karen's on top of things!" replied the rustic voice from the speaker.

"Thank you," she said.

"See you shortly," said Bill, switching off the phone.

* * *

A short while later they arrived at the gates to the reservation. Nathan was waiting to guide them to the cabin, talking quietly to the Indian police.

The dimly lit streets made their arrival harrowing. Shadows formed by the moving vehicle slid silently over the repeatedly similar housing, each dwelling containing no less than three dogs. It was with considerable relief that they finally closed the door, silencing the barking of the hundreds of hounds warning that strangers had entered their domain.

"Bill, you're a sight for sore eyes!" said Dusty quickly moving to shake his hand.

"Likewise big fella, I'm so glad to be here!" Bill said. "Sorry, I didn't mean to be rude. I'd like you to formally meet Peta. Younger sister to Carlos!"

Dusty seemed lost for words as he stood towering over Peta, a vibrant passion became real as their eyes met. He moved and shook her gently by the hand with tenderness in his touch she had not known since the early years of her late husband. She craved the affections of yesteryear and never thought they could once again be realized. But Dusty had somehow crossed the bridge to her emotions rekindling the long dormant flames of passion. Looking deep into the eyes of this rugged man standing before her, she felt the softness in his touch, warming the depth of her soul.

"How was your journey?" the big man asked, his mouth becoming dry as he searched for the words, looking at Peta standing innocently next to Linda.

"Very comfortable, thank you!" replied Peta, her voice trying to disguise the passion in her eyes. "Could I please see my brother?" she said with urgency in her tone, eagerly looking up at the rugged stranger. His eyes a pale shade of blue, expressed hidden feelings he thought he was not capable of expressing.

"In the morning!" replied Dusty as the bedroom door creaked open. "He's not been well all day. He really needs the rest!"

A young woman rose to her feet as the group entered the room.

"Peta, I would like you to meet Karen!" said Dusty, his hand trembling as he placed it on the small of Peta's back.

"Karen's been helping Carlos and the people on the reservation since we arrived!" His voice seemed even drier and he was finding difficulty trying to swallow.

"Karen, I cannot thank you enough!" Peta replied. Both girls moved beyond hearing range as the small talk continued.

During dinner, Bill couldn't help notice the fascination Dusty held for Peta and she for him. In the fleeting moment that had passed since their first meeting the two had become inseparable, their eyes constantly searching for the other with a passion defying words.

With the night growing late Dusty and Peta departed the cabin arm in arm, again disturbing the dogs but returning a short time later.

"Problem?" asked Bill standing talking to Nathan's father as Dusty and Peta quickly closed the door behind them.

"I think so. The vehicle you arrived in has a satellite link. They know exactly where we are!" said Dusty, his arm firmly around Peta.

"No way, we took all the precautions!" replied Bill in a highly defensive tone.

"Bill! No one is blaming you. The Rover had been wired well before you left San Francisco!" replied Dusty.

"You're kidding, right?" said Linda wrapped tight in the Indian blanket Nathan had presented to her earlier. "How on earth did you spot the wire?"

"I didn't! Peta caught the red light flashing intermittently on the ground directly beneath the vehicle!" replied Dusty as Nathan and Saara moved outside to see for themselves.

"Can you dismantle it?" asked Bill with everyone now back in the cabin, closing the door to the noise of the dogs.

"Not a chance. Any interference to remove the link usually ends in some form of detonation!" replied Dusty.

"Then what can we do?" asked Linda, the same question on everyone's lips.

"Nothing, it's much too late anyway. We'll leave in the morning. I really don't want to involve these innocent people in our affairs," replied Dusty, meaning the danger to the Apache, seemingly unperturbed by the situation as he and Peta again departed outside.

He and she walking arm in arm talked the small talk of newly found lovers. They whispered sweet nothings of the past and present, laughing lovingly at each other's jokes. Peta felt she'd finally found the person with whom she would grow old as they strolled beneath the shimmering stars for hours then just before first light, returned to the silence of the cabin. Inside they were met by Nathan's uncle who informed Dusty that this was possibly the safest place to be and they were welcome to stay as long as they liked.

"Thank you Little Wolf!" said Dusty.   "But hiding is not going to answer our questions."

"Stay! At least until you find Great, Great Grandfather" replied Little Wolf.

"I will not put your people to the test! The people we are dealing with are vicious and desperate. But we thank you!" replied Dusty sincerely with Peta also nodding approval.

Chapter 25

The morning was an experience to encounter. The bright yellow glow of the desert glistened with the heat of the morning sun, casting a shimmering array of colours delicately upon the surrounding canyon walls. This turned the disturbing feelings of the night to the majestic splendour of the spiritual sensing flashing around the canyon with the dead from the past, dancing to the rhythm of the living.

Peta, kneeling beside Carlos, whispering a silent prayer, had tears in her eyes as there was no response from the frail figure lying motionless on the bed before her. Karen could do nothing further to help except ease the suffering with injections of morphine, hopefully relieving some of the life-sapping pain passing through his body. The AIDS virus had taken its toll, not much remained but skin and bone. The once proud body surrendering, giving back the life to god and forever branded a homosexual by the way he died. The shock came as they quietly sat in the outside room feeling for Carlos, his life rapidly ebbing away.

"The person lying in that room is not my brother!" said Peta.

"Peta, what are you saying?" replied Bill, her surprising revelation's reverberating around the room.

"Bill, I'm telling you. That man is not Carlos! He's not my brother!" replied Peta, her voice filled with a sorrow.

"My brother was born with a defining heart-shaped birthmark on the left side of his neck. This person does not possess that mark."

"But the fingerprints Mick lifted," replied Dusty. "Are those of your brother Carlos? And he seems to know the complete inner workings of the Bureau!"

"I don't know who you have in that room. I only know he's not Carlos!" Her emotions were becoming confused as she once again had lost her brother.

"Then it's time to find out what's gone wrong," replied Bill as Karen entered the room with tears streaming down her face.

"He's gone," she whispered, her hands shaking and the colour visibly drained from her cheeks, trying desperately to hold back her emotions. Bill noticing her sorrow moved quickly to comfort her through the moment but Linda was already in her arms, together both girls weeping quite unashamedly.

The frail remains had finally succumbed to the virus. The life force that once flowed proudly through the veins was now extinguished. The purpose of life passed to the next level was the Apache saying.

* * *

The following morning was a cold grey, cloudy day. The rain had been falling steadily throughout the night with the sinister southwesterly wind sweeping forcefully off the plains. The weather, as wicked as it was, didn't deter the people from gathering outside the cabin as soon as the word had circulated across the reservation about the passing of the small man with the virus. He had departed this life only to join the elders of a bygone era, the Human Beings.

Nathan, dressed and painted in the traditional way, proudly placed the body of 73 on the prepared burial rack for the ceremony ahead. Saara wore the softer look, her all-white suede dress and high-lace moccasins, looked extremely vulnerable chanting incantations with the women of the reservation as Nathan pounded the drums. Food, drink and weapons had been placed on the burial rack for his long journey to the hereafter as Chief Little Wolf lit the fire signalling the start of the voyage. The ceremony lasted all day and long into the night.

By late afternoon the following day, their affairs in order, they headed back to San Francisco. Nathan's grandfather still eluded them, for while cleansing the soul the body became invisible to earthly sightings, or so the legend went. And who could chase a ghost!

Chapter 26

Bill was driving quickly through the canyons, a smile on his face, staring into the infinite emptiness of the desert, comforting thoughts crossing his mind.

"What are you smiling at?" Linda asked, her voice a half whisper.

"Nothing, just thinking," replied Bill, his eyes still glued on the road ahead and not wanting to answer her question.

"About what?" she persisted, her mind wandering to the quiet pond of Haiti.

"Truly, nothing darling!" the smile remained.

"Go on. Tell me!" she insisted, with the others listening intently to their whispered conversation.

"Tell her!" taunted Dusty from the back seat as Peta jabbed him in the ribs with her elbow.

"Don't be rude!" said Peta with Nathan and Saara quietly smiling at the stunned look on Dusty's face.

"A thought," interrupted Linda. "What about the link?" she said, turning to face Dusty, still rubbing his ribs vigorously.

"Relax! I've set up a static field to hopefully nullify their signal," replied Dusty.

"Hopefully?" said Linda with everyone's attention now directed at Dusty. "Explain to me how that works?" she said looking the big man directly in the eye.

"Simple! I couldn't disarm it, so I tried the next best thing. I scattered it digitally using some magnets from an old generator lying idle at the back of Nathans uncle's lean-to," he replied.

"What if some prick pushes the button?" asked Bill, the question no one wanted to ask.

"With any luck, nothing. By using magnets the signal becomes too weak to trace. A kind of force field," said Dusty.

"Again hopefully!" replied Linda but smiling as she caught the love in Peta's eyes.

"There are no guarantees, not in this world. And definitely not with the people we are dealing with. If it hasn't been activated by now and I'm sure they would be trying, then I don't think we have a problem!" replied Dusty, his arm firmly around Peta.

"Great work you old bastard!" quipped Linda quietly, feeling a tremendous relief at the big man's knowledge.

"Enough of the old!" replied Dusty.

Incredible. Is there nothing this man can't do? thought Linda, turning up the radio, with the road ahead seemingly endless.

Chapter 27

In the time away, Mick moved all their equipment to a grand old mansion located deeper into the San Francisco valley. There were two large Rottweilers patrolling the outside perimeter. The windows and doors were fitted with electronic pressure switches making unwanted entry almost impossible. The heavy steel gates, fully automated, opened only on command from the main house. Security cameras fitted to wide cam screened all visitors showing recorded close-ups of anyone coming or going.

San Francisco loomed large in the distance, her Golden Gate standing high above the bay, the sea filling the wide mouthed opening with U.S. Naval ships moored leisurely around the harbor. Today, San Francisco was bathed in warm rays of sunlight protruding intermittently from behind clouds that would race their vehicle across town.

Approaching the outskirts of the city, Howard rang Bill on the hands free cell phone informing them of their new location, but before he could complete his sentence Linda interrupted.

"Dad, why the sudden move? We were quite comfortable at mum's?"

"This one's been paid for by KWB. Hamish thought that with your crowd and the assaults on your persons it would be safer moving everyone in together," replied

Howard. "Besides this new place has unparalleled security and loads of room. And we both felt that the time was right."

"Mum's back!" replied Linda smiling at her father's attempt to humour her.

"That, too!"

"Ok. Thanks dad. We'll ring when we get there!" said Linda switching off the cell.

"Where to?" asked Bill.

"I'll just check the map! But I think I know where we are heading!" explained Linda with her detailed knowledge of the city.

* * *

Arriving at the house a little after four, they were greeted by Mick's familiar voice, the gates opening slowly as the young ones stepped watchfully from the vehicle then closing behind them with a thunderous clang. The Rover moved slowly towards the house. A magnificent marble staircase dominated the splendour of the stately old mansion. In the rearview mirror Bill could see Nathan and Saara familiarizing themselves with the area, the dogs quick to intercept the new intruders but instantly Saara had them eating out of her hand as though she had known them since pups.

"How was the trip? How is Carlos?" asked Mick, standing at the top of the stairs, feeling like Rhett Butler, from *"Gone with the Wind."*

"Slow down," said Linda, moving slowly towards him, her travel bags hanging from both arms with her skirt heavily wrinkled from the trip.

"How in the hell did you find this place?" asked Dusty, following Linda closely up the capacious marble stairs.

"I didn't," said Mick. "Howard and Hamish organized everything. I merely moved our gear over. And I think you'll all be pleasantly surprised with your rooms."

"Pretty lavish!" said Bill, looking over the premises whilst locking up the Rover.

"You don't need to lock the car. At least not inside the gates!" said Mick smiling as he'd longed for their company and the messy conversations he often had with Linda.

"Old habits die hard" replied Bill at awe with the spacious surrounds.

"You certainly can't call Hamish cheap!" laughed Mick, who himself still hadn't come to terms with the luxury afforded them. "You think this is good. Wait till you see the inside." He began to help the girls with their luggage.

"It's gorgeous!" Linda said, stopping at the top of the stairs, observing the huge spacious lawns with the superbly manicured gardens around the perimeter. The pool was breathtakingly beautiful, not only by the colour of the tiles, but the quality of the water combined with the clarity, left nothing to desire. The plush deck chairs scattered liberally around the pool made for an inviting scenario.

* * *

Night arrived quickly as always and with dinner cleared away everyone settled comfortably around the open fire, Mick quietly playing the harmonica to the crackling of burning logs and Dusty and Peta cuddled up on the lounge listening, while making small talk. The room was filled with comforting familiar sounds as the dark often heralded the onset of the fog bringing the curtain rolling in to blanket an area, releasing the demons of the night.

"Mick what are your possible worst fears?" asked Bill, taking everyone by surprise and shattering the tranquillity of the moment. The glow from the fire flickered deep on the walls, at times changing the colours of the room from a light pastel to a deeper red.

"What do you mean?" replied Mick, placing the harmonica on the table next to the lounge.

"Hypothetically speaking, what is the one thing you fear in life?" Bill said.

"I've never thought about it!" replied Mick, stopping to collect his thoughts. "I suppose, speaking hypothetically, not being able to access a coded classified area in any one corporate computer! That would be the worst," he said, looking at Karen who had only just entered the room.

"Do you always think computers?" asked Linda. "Don't you ever think of normal things?"

"Such as?" replied Mick.

"Women!" she snapped.

"Bill asked my worst fears, not my alternate fears," replied Mick, completely and utterly confused but smiling.

"Chauvinist!" muttered Linda.

"Linda! I grew up with a house full of women, and as such I think I've earned the right," replied Mick. "But what brought this on?"

"The other day, Howard asked me to help finish a story about people's hidden fears. Interestingly enough, the least had to do with violent crime," replied Bill, as Nathan excused himself and headed for the comfort of bed.

"Then what's your fear?" asked Linda, sitting comfortably in Bill's lap.

"That's easy, drowning! It haunts me. For some unknown reason, I've always been afraid of water. I sometimes have nightmares of things wrapping tightly around my ankles and dragging me under in some murky slimy river!" replied Bill with Linda shuddering as a cold shiver crept up her spine then Peta moved closer to their conversation.

"Then what are your fears, Peta?" asked Linda, the flickering flames reflecting in her hair.

Peta didn't answer directly. Her shyness kept her emotions locked deep within her mind.

"Peta, we're all friends," said Linda, not meaning to pry but probing for an answer.

"Ever since Carlos disappeared all those years ago, I dread being alone. Both our parents being dead, and my only other relative, my younger sister, was tragically killed two years ago in an automobile accident," replied Peta, the tears of old memories in her eyes.

"I'm sorry, Peta. I didn't mean to pry," said Linda, reaching out to comfort her.

"And what are your fears, Dusty?" asked Mick, trying purposely to remove the attention from Peta.

"I don't have any. At least, not since meeting this young lady," replied Dusty emanating signs of emotions as Peta moved closer to hug him.

"That's sweet," whispered Linda, wrapping her arms lovingly around Bill.

"Then what are your fears?" Peta asked softly, her eyes cast towards Linda.

"Cancer," she quietly replied. "I dread the disease. The body slowly devoured from within. Tissues internally

rotting and we only find out about it when it's too late."
Tears formed in her eyes, fuelled by emotions of despair.

"Is cancer common in your family?" asked Dusty
quietly, holding Peta's hand gently in his and stroking her
long black hair from her face.

"No!" replied Linda.

"Then you have no fears. Cancer is mostly genetically
inherited," said Mick. He began playing his harmonica
once more as the phone rang.

"Rather late to be ringing!" said Dusty moving to pick
up the receiver.

"I think you have something of mine and I would like
it returned. Immediately!" came the cold callous voice over
the open speaker installed on all the phones earlier by
Mick.

"Who is this?" replied Dusty, half expecting an answer.

"Never mind, return the box you have, and return it
unopened!" the voice commanded and the phone went
dead.

"Was that Carlos?" Dusty asked Peta.

"No. The voice sounded more like Victor!" she replied.

"You mean Ramos!" said Dusty.

"Yes! But he is in no-way the same person I knew in
Haiti!" replied Peta with a look of fear in her eyes.

"The person you knew in Haiti never existed. Ramos
was only using you to get to your brother!" said Mick.

"For some unknown reason the man thinks we know
too much!" replied Dusty. "And tell me this! How did he
know about the box?"

"I think it's time we found out what he knows! Only
then will we know what he knows. Or something along
those lines!" continued Dusty.

"Linda, the box you guys found in Peta's shop. Do you still have it?" Dusty asked.

"I'd forgotten all about it. Yes I think it's still in my travel bag," she replied, leaving the room but returning a short time later with the small box firmly in hand.

Dusty, with little effort and the help of his Bowie knife hanging trustily by his side, flicked open the lid as everyone moved for in close for a better look at the contents. The small box contained a miniature spool of film, and something wrapped tightly in old newspaper clippings.

"What is it?" inquired Linda, moving ever nearer.

"It's an old microfilm," replied Mick.

"Show me," said Linda, for her view had been blocked by the mass of bodies trying to see for themselves.

Dusty handed Mick the spool then proceeded to unwrap the paper around the mystery object.

"A key!" said Linda. "I wonder where it belongs?" She looked up at Dusty who had a concerned look on his face.

"Mick, do you possess anything in your bag of tricks that would let us view this microfilm film?" asked Dusty, a note of urgency in his voice.

"Sure! I'll run the spool through the micro processor. She'll handle it. I'll need to make a few adjustments and add a couple of bits. Then we should be ready to rock and roll in no time!" replied Mick, studying the key with the letters SIMB 66 stamped to the side. "What do you suppose the symbols stand for?" he said.

"Could we please see the micro film tonight?" interrupted Dusty, looking down at the key held firmly in Mick's hand.

"I'll be a little while!" Mick replied as he left the room to pick up his bits and pieces.

"Not a problem!" said Dusty then there was a loud knock at the door.

The security systems hadn't activated and the dogs were unusually quiet, yet there was the knock again! Carefully, Dusty reached for the 9mm automatic strapped loosely under his left arm as Nathan, who had returned to the room, moved swiftly to cover him from the opposite doorway, with Saara taking a cross position.

Everyone waited nervously in the silence of the room, only the crackling of the fire could be heard in the distance. Then the knock came again, only this time, deafeningly loud.

Cautiously, Dusty swung open the door and as he did, in stepped the biggest, blackest African Bill had ever laid eyes on. He felt a sense of fear when the intruder looked in his direction. The tingling of the spine was only relieved when Dusty spoke.

"Clint! You old bastard! What took you so long?" said Dusty slipping the gun back in its holster.

"I only just received word you were in some trouble," replied the newcomer with his dark brown eyes looking closely at the company around him.

"How did you get through the gates?" asked Mick returning to the room with his bits and pieces in hand, closely eyeing the huge figure now standing in the light of the hall.

"The dogs! What were they doing?" said Linda, standing confidently behind Bill.

"Come in. Meet the gang!" said Dusty closing the door to the cool of the evening air.

"People, I would like to introduce Clint Halliday! Presidential bodyguard in the sixties and seventies!" said Dusty, bursting with pride that his friend had finally come.

"Easy, Dusty I'm still active!" Clint replied, when Karen joined the group from the dark of the back balcony.

"How the hell did you locate us?" asked Dusty, finding it hard to remove the smile from his face.

"All these questions and I thought you were the ones in trouble!" replied Clint.

"Seriously, how did you make it through the gates without setting off the alarm?" said Mick.

"Friend!" said Clint, looking to Mick.

"The name's Mick," he replied, his eyes not leaving the floor.

"Sorry! I didn't mean to be rude" replied Clint. "Finding you was easy. You don't enter high risk security levels without attracting attention."

"Then they know who we are!" said Mick.

"No! No one officially suspects anything. And as for getting in, the gates are wide open. And dogs, I didn't see any!" replied Clint looking to Dusty for an explanation.

Nathan quickly slipped out the back and Saara the front, both returning almost immediately.

"What's wrong?" asked Dusty, with Clint standing close by his side.

"The dogs, they've been poisoned," replied Nathan, moving swiftly to the kitchen in search of salt.

"Are they dead?" asked Linda, following Nathan closely.

"No! Saara may have got to them early enough"; replied Nathan, the salt and a bowl of warm water in hand as he hurried back to Saara.

"The dogs, they're highly trained. They wouldn't accept food from a stranger!" said Linda, again joining Dusty and Clint at the top of the stairs, watching Saara frantically trying to save both dogs.

"Perhaps not a stranger," replied Clint.

"What do you mean by that?" she asked.

"Just what I said!" said Clint in a tone which ended the conversation. "Do you have any idea of the people you who are dealing with?" he said, as Linda shrugging her shoulders from the cold air, moved back inside joining Bill by the fire.

"Do the names Ramos and Prodi ring any bells?" asked Dusty, the two moving back inside to where Mick had set the decoder in readiness for the showing.

"How the hell did you get involved with that bunch?" queried Clint.

"Not by choice, I assure you! Yet somehow it just happened," replied Dusty.

"Off the record, I've personally been after the bastards for the past fourteen years, but they're hard to track down. Every time I finally locate one of them, they anticipate my every move!"

"I know the feeling" replied Dusty as Mick declared the decoder ready to go.

"And what's this?" asked Clint, looking curiously at the equipment.

"It's a long story! I'll clue you in as we roll," replied Dusty then the screen sprang to life. Carlos was speaking directly to the camera. Bill glanced over at Peta sitting on a barstool, her hands clutched tightly in her lap with the tears rolling silently down her cheeks. As Dusty closely watched the screen he moved quietly behind her, a comforting hand placed gently on each shoulder.

Chapter 28

"If you're viewing this film, God willing I'm dead. I don't think J. Edgar Hoover knows the film exists. Only my close friend Ramos whom once I trusted knows of the film.

"Everything that's happened began in late '67. We had been sent on a disruptive mission to Haiti. Their government of the day was giving Washington a hard time and threatening to swing over to Castro and the Communist way. At the time America was exploiting the small island as the main power base for all movements in and around Cuba. Nuclear warheads aimed at Havana and Moscow were located throughout the country. Our orders were 'to quickly discredit the Haitian government and replace it with people loyal to our cause.

"The exercise took less than three months to complete. On our return home, Victoria brought with her three small apes. Two were males and one female to which she had become extremely attached during our visit to Haiti. A month after returning home two of the tiny apes fell ill. Significantly the sick ones were homosexually inclined with the female remaining completely unaffected. For some reason she was completely immune to their disease. Victoria moved the monkeys to the Hoover Institute of Advanced Research and Technology in the hope that Henderson, the head of the experimental section could *assist in finding a cure and prevent the disease from gradually killing the males.*

"When one of the baboons died, Hoover who had visited the hospital from time to time and observed the homosexual tendencies of the male apes, asked Henderson if a similar human strain could be duplicated. The truth being Hoover himself was an active homosexual who hated his feelings towards other men. He envisaged that by eradicating the homosexual, his feelings towards them would dissipate and he could lead a normal life without the homosexual tendencies.

"Henderson didn't question the orders but moved quickly using all available resources under the code name 'Cleansing' endeavouring to genetically change the monkey virus into a human strain. But things moved slowly for Henderson and tensions started to surface. Washington began asking questions and it became harder and harder to conceal the usage of funds.

"The following eight months Antonio and I were stationed in Columbia aligning the drug lords of the country, guaranteeing that we had first use of their services should the need arise. It also ensured that the buckets of money they donated generously towards Henderson's research would not stop. In return, the FBI, lead by Hoover and his hit squad would turn a blind eye towards certain ships importing heroin and cocaine into the States via San Francisco.

"Upon returning home from Columbia eight months, later I learned of a certain Doctor Farnsworth, an English professor brought specifically to America by J. Edgar to develop a radical new genetic implantation as the methods used by Henderson in his research the past

months, had met only with mild success. But when Farnsworth introduced bacterial engineering, the breakthrough finally came.

"They had somehow developed a new virus with the twenty two chromosomes needed to make it human remaining dormant in the body's immune system for up to six years. The new strain was transferred by body fluids. It was completely undetectable by the known available tests of the day and was highly contagious on all counts throughout the dormant period, guaranteeing maximum exposure towards the homosexual. The new virus ensured a complete immune systems break down. The vast numbers of active homosexuals who vanished from San Francisco over the early years were used as guinea pigs in the development of the virus at the Hoover institute. No-one survived. The authorities in that period couldn't care less. No one took any notice. Those who vanished were part of the permissive society and carefully selected by Victoria.

"The only inquiries about the missing came from their lovers. But being homosexuals themselves lessened their cause.

"The frightening part of this document is that I fully believed that what we were doing was right. I never asked what Hoover was doing. I'm as guilty as he was!

"The homosexual ideals in late '69 ascended to indecent levels. They convinced me we were 'cleansing' mankind of God's unnatural acts. A complete and total merciful genocide in the name of mankind."

The film stopped abruptly as the light from the screen flashed wildly around the room.

"Jesus!" gasped Bill.   "What have these assholes done?"

There was not a murmur in the room. The silence could be cut with a knife as the reality of the enormity of the greatest genocide ever started was realized.

Dusty was shaking his head and Peta was sitting quietly, tears now streaming down her face but crying in silence.

"Is that it, Mick?" asked Dusty trying to console Peta as she hopelessly shed her tears.

"No! The film broke. It's shitloads old!" he replied, trying hurriedly to repair the damage.

"Can the fucker be fixed?" asked Clint, moving slowly to the phone.

"Sure! Only take seconds," replied Mick, rewinding the spool and placing it back in the decoder.

"Bobbie! You'd best get over here! I don't care! Make time," said Clint into the phone.   "It's extremely important!" he said giving directions then hanging up the phone. The astonishment at the abruptness of the call caught everyone by surprise.

"Ready," said Mick the old film flickering once more with the discoloration telling its age as Carlos continued.

"The reason I have gone along with these people is self explanatory. When the Republicans legalized homosexuality meaning votes in late '68, all hell broke loose!

"In New York, Fire Island has become the Mecca. Upwards of three thousand men per day visit there openly displaying their sodomy of each other.

"In San Francisco, Castro Street with the bathhouses packed with men, the exchange of sexual partners

numbering dozens per day has become the norm. The piers and harbour meeting places were filled with acts once only exposed behind locked doors, but had now moved to the open, displayed publicly."

The old film showed the men kissing and fondling each other, bathing and openly exchanging partners whilst waving to the camera. Perpetuity had replaced modesty, the unnatural side of man unleashing passions suppressed for so long but now legally displayed.

The film flashed to the Hoover Institute, showing patients with numbers tattooed on their foreheads, aimlessly wandering the darkened corridors.

"Since congress amended the Act towards the homosexual, their numbers have swelled, threatening man's very existence. Gayton Dugas, a Canadian airline steward was carefully selected to release the new strain to his partners, the virus we now call AIDS. The new strain was secretly administered with the toxin containing the virus during his inoculation for his world travels. He was now free to spread the plague amongst the gay society. The same strain was released six months earlier into Central Africa to test the antidote that Farnsworth said he had developed. And I suspect that if anything went wrong with the virus, Africa was to blame.

"Zaire seemed safe, the experiment showed signs of failure and I was shocked to learn later that two hundred and seventy four, men women and children had perished due to a new killer disease. The entire village was wiped out in only a matter of weeks. The new virus was supposedly created by the men of that village sexually molesting the local baboons. That was the story spread by

the FBI, but I know this to be untrue, and now realize that the antidote Henderson used in Africa mutated the new strain to a higher level, transcending the AIDS virus a thousand fold.

"By first releasing the virus into a third world country, it assured everyone the strain was unmistakably created out of Central Africa, and not on home soil. The scientists and doctors researching the virus in those days were led to believe by the FBI and CIA that a species of chimpanzee found in the Congo carried the same virus that was now killing the gays. They blamed the local aborigines who caught and butchered the apes for their meat for the creation of the virus. The jump of the virus to man was supposedly caused by the blood from the slain monkeys and the blood of their captors mingling during the course of the slaughter.

"What a load of crap. The slaughter has been going on for centuries but now we are led to believe what they want us to believe. The truth is that we started the virus, not them. As in them, I mean the locals. Take a close look at the genetics between man and ape and you will have your answer."

They sat silently listening to Carlos, not wanting to believe what they were hearing, but the horrendous revelations continued.

"I was assured by Farnsworth that the virus could be terminated at any point in time with the antidote housed at the Institute. It never, in my wildest dreams occurred to me they were lying. I remained loyal to the cause throughout the seventies and early eighties, but with the death toll now steadily climbing, the infighting began. I *blame Ramos and Prodi for the burning of the institute and the deaths of everyone involved, leaving no evidence other than this film to show the atrocities that happened there. The supposed antidotes also vanished and with females, children and haemophiliacs now contracting the virus, things became frightening.*

"When Peter Scott, a close friend and colleague, threatened to expose the truth to a senate committee, he, his wife and three young children were callously murdered, their car exploding in the driveway of their home as they were preparing to leave for their annual vacation. I knew then it was time to disappear. These people are evil."

The old film flickered to a close. The room remained deadly silent, with the light from the decoder flickering brightly on the ceiling as the alarm to the main gates sounded.

"That's Robert," said Clint quietly but there was no response from the faces around the room as they reflected tragically on the revelations made by Carlos.

"The fucking assholes did it!" yelled Mick, his voice reverberating off the walls. "The murdering bastards actually did it!" He sat down next to Linda, shaking his head violently.

"Could someone, anyone please open the gate?" repeated Clint, as the alarm again sounded. A short time later there was a heavy knock at the door with Dusty moving to respond and Clint close by his side flicking on the outside lights transforming night into day.

"Bobbie! Glad you could come," said Clint as a small man entered the room flanked by two agents wearing standard issue FBI dark suits and reflective glasses.

"I didn't think I had a choice," was the reply then Clint introduced the man to the gathering.

"Guys! Let me introduce Robert Muller. Robert is a friend, work mate and compatriot. We have known each other the past twenty years, and I personally will do anything that Bobby asks, without question. And I'm sure the claim is reciprocated!"

Clint looked around the room at everyone gathered closely together. No one answered but the tension was thick and heavy.

The trio shuffled into the kitchen where their meeting lasted but a few moments. When Dusty handed Bobby the spool, he and the other two in dark glasses left without a sound breaking the silence, with only the movement of the pebbles shuffling beneath the wheels as the limo slowly moved off.

"What's happening?" asked Peta, her eyes red from the countless tears shed over her brother's involvement in the eradication of life.

"Nothing sweetheart!" replied Dusty, himself with a lump to the throat as he held her close.

"Robert Muller is the director of the FBI here in San Francisco. He will view the film in its entirety then get back to us," said Clint, yawning slightly for the night had become extremely late.

"This clipping the key was wrapped in! It's an obituary," said Mick, holding the piece of paper in his hand.

"What's it say?" asked Linda, moving to turn up the lights.

"In the memory of James McCall. Tragically killed, June 2 1972. He lost his life unselfishly trying to free a young female victim from a car wreck. Both were incinerated," read Mick.

"What's that writing down the border?" asked Linda, peering over Mick's shoulders, her arms resting comfortably around his neck.

"It says simply, 'James was right'," replied Mick.

"About what?" asked Linda.

"Could I see that?" asked Bill, his hand outstretched to Mick. "I remember reading an article James wrote on the Hoover institute in early '72. He made claims of human injustices, secret experimental programs and staff conveniently killed in unrelated accidents, the complete mess covered up by the FBI."

"And you think James confirms Carlos' revelations?" said Linda, looking closely at Bill.

"Absolutely!" replied Clint slowly coming to terms with the Carlos admissions.

"And you doubt it was an accident that claimed James' life?" asked Linda of Bill.

"No question about it! He too was murdered," he replied.

"And you think these people will kill again," she said

"Absolutely and without hesitation! Ramos and Prodi are in way too deep to stop now! Can you possibly imagine the consequences of an unsuspecting world getting wind of a handful of lunatics changing the course of history!" replied Bill. "Eradicating tens if not hundreds of millions?"

Nothing further was mentioned of the disclosures perpetrated on the film. Each felt a pain in different ways. Some of Linda's best friends were gay and she treasured those friendships and guarded them jealously, whereas Dusty, being a man's man held no time for the homosexual but wouldn't move to harm them.

The radio in the background had a country and western tune playing when Dusty once more broke the silence.

"Linda! You and Peta will have to vanish. It might be a good idea if Howard went with you!" he said.

"You know Dad! He wouldn't leave the magazine!" replied Linda.

"He doesn't have a choice," said Clint.

"Then you tell him," she replied defiantly, her eyes not leaving his as she moved to the kitchen.

"Shush, listen!" said Mick, hurriedly moving to turn up the volume on the radio.

"There has been an explosion at the Courier," came the news flash blaring from the speakers. "No details are yet available, but the San Francisco Fire Department now has the blaze contained!"

"What's happened?" asked Linda, moving back into the room, staring at the blank faces looking back at her. "Have I missed something?"

"At the moment, we're not sure what's transpired," the announcer continued, "But there's extensive damage to the building."

"Mick, is he talking about Dad?" Linda demanded, a quiver in her voice as Bill moved to hold her.

"Yes! I think so," replied Mick, his eyes not leaving the carpet.

"I must get over there," she said pushing away from Bill then grabbing her coat and hurrying to the door.

"I'll come with you!" yelled Peta, following Linda in close pursuit.

"Hold everything!" replied Clint. "If the worst has happened, there's not a thing you can do, except expose yourself on their terms. And that's exactly what they're after."

Linda was weeping, tears flowing freely from her soft, pale blue eyes.

"You can only help Howard by helping yourself," said Bill, knowing this would do little to comfort her through the moment. As he again moved to hold her, the phone rang.

"Linda! It's your father!" said Mick, smiling and then handing her the phone.

"Dad, I thought you were dead!" she said as Peta moved close, her arms firmly around Linda's waist. "Where are you? Well, stay there. Clint and Dusty are just about to leave. "They'll pick you up on the way," she said, hanging up the receiver.

"He's with Hamish at the station!" said Linda, slowly brushing the tears from her eyes, holding tightly on to Peta.

"Don't worry! We'll bring him home," replied Clint, returning his gun to its holster after carefully checking each chamber.

Chapter 29

It was three a.m. by the time they arrived at the Courier only to witness the complete devastation of the first floor. Every window was destroyed, the blast shattering glass half a block away. Bricks and metal fittings were strewn amongst the fire hoses snaking their way towards the building. The fire had long since been extinguished, although the smell of smouldering foam lingered thick in the air.

"Unbelievable," said Dusty looking at the destruction. "I nursed some of these kids when they were babies! This didn't have to happen." The emotion was heavy in his voice as he stood looking up at the rubble that was once the offices of the Weekly.

"No, it didn't!" said Clint, himself shocked at the lengths these people had now gone to.

Dusty's eyes closely searched the small crowd which had gathered at the end of the street, but saw no faces he recognized as he and Clint quickly departed the scene.

* * *

Arriving at KWB they were met in the foyer by Sally and led directly to Hamish's large plush office surrounded by glass windows and pictures of the ancient Apache, Geronimo dotting the walls. Dusty introduced Clint to Hamish and Howard but it took some time for Howard to settle as he didn't feel comfortable while being in the presence of a black man. He had been raised the Southern way - respect the Negro by all means, but don't trust him.

"I believe you were President Kennedy's personal body guard?" asked Howard, exploiting his 'I'm looking down at you' tone.

"Affirmative," replied Clint, guarding his reply carefully.

"What went wrong?" replied Howard.

"Clint is here to help," quipped Hamish as he could no longer tolerate the blatant put down of a man here to offer assistance at his own expense.

"Sorry! But someone has killed eleven of my people!" replied Howard. "Somebody has to be accountable."

"And someone will be," replied Clint in a reassuring voice.

"What happened?" asked Hamish, shocked by the current events.

"Somebody allowed a bomb into the building," replied Clint, looking at Dusty for confirmation.

"None of my people, I hope?" asked Howard.

"No I don't think so," answered Dusty.

"Can these bastards be stopped?" said Howard, glancing into Clint's dark eyes.

"Anyone can be stopped!" said Clint. "But not the way you're going!"

"Then how?" asked Hamish, urgency now showing on his face. Then Dusty interrupted informing the two men of the film they had viewed then handed it to Robert Muller of the FBI.

"But these people, aren't they FBI?" asked Howard.

"They were! But their files terminated in '87," replied Dusty.

"Then you don't believe the FBI is involved?" said Hamish.

"I'm sure of it," replied Dusty. "Clint's part of the new Bureau."

"It's not like you think," said Clint. "Let me explain a few truths! When Kennedy was shot, the White House suspected an internal conspiracy by J. Edgar and certain members of the FBI. Congress ordered a full investigation but the congressional committee investigating came up empty. Evidence vanished, people involved were killed and all the incriminating files erased."

He looked at the faces listening attentively.

"Lee Harvey Oswald who was murdered by Jack Ruby who in-turn was shot dead by federal agents closely associated with Hoover had worked in Russia the past two years for the FBI," continued Clint.

"You're telling me that Oswald was a federal agent. That he was FBI and ordered murdered by Hoover?" asked Howard.

"Jack Ruby was murdered by the mafia of the day by direct orders from the CIA who were in bed with Hoover!" said Clint.

"Can this be proven?" asked Howard.

"I can only speculate. But the evidence now suggests that that was what happened for the stakes were extremely high and Kennedy had to go. As did Bobby," said Clint looking at Dusty for further confirmation.

"You didn't answer my question! Were Oswald and Ruby FBI agents?" repeated Howard.

"Oswald had worked for the FBI in Russia and had only just returned to America the week before the assignation. I don't know what he was doing on the sixth floor that fatal day, but I do know he wasn't the shooter. Jack Ruby was J. Edgar's puppet and closely associated with the mafia," replied Clint. "Jack would do whatever it took to please Hoover such was the fear of the man they called boss. You have to remember that J. Edgar had secret files on every high-ranking official and threatened to use that information against them."

Everybody was still attentive.

"When Ramos and Prodi mysteriously vanished the Bureau tried to pension off Savage, but failed miserably," continued Clint.

"Then Savage still retains access to the computer?" said Hamish.

"Oh yeah," replied Clint.

"Could he then be the one erasing the files?" asked Hamish.

"No! Savage is here in San Francisco. The erasures came from Washington," answered Clint.

"Washington?" asked Howard. "What part of Washington?"

"That we don't know! Whoever erased the Central computer entered through a series of computers, much the same way Mick did, virtually untraceable," said Clint.

"Then what's our next step?" asked Howard.

"Flush them out! Make them come to us," replied Dusty, looking across at Hamish sitting partially behind his desk, puffing lightly on a dollar Cuban.

"How?" asked Howard

"Using the computer and the inquisitiveness of human nature, they'll come," said Dusty with Howard slowly nodding approval.

Chapter 30

Howard was warmly met at the door by Linda, the tears in her eyes painfully evident.

"I thought I'd lost you," she said with Howard brushing the hair gently from her face and delicately drying her eyes.

"I'm all right!" he replied. "But we have lost some good people tonight!"

It was he who instigated the extra hours in trying to meet deadlines for the magazine. Normally the cut off point was midnight and had that been the case, his friends would still be alive.

"Howard, are you all right with what's happened?" asked Dusty, observing the emptiness in his eyes.

"I can't understand how these people are always one step ahead of us," replied Howard, turning to Dusty for confirmation.

"That has been a huge problem, but soon everything will be revealed!" answered Clint as Howard placed his arm over Clint's shoulder trying to make up for the rudeness shown earlier in Hamish's office.

"If everything goes to plan, we should get a good look at our adversaries shortly," concluded Clint as the early morning sun peaked through the huge, stained glass window facing east.

* * *

Mick and Dusty were at the old house completing the final touches when Clint finally rang.

"Ready?" Clint asked, preparing himself for the moments ahead. Karen, in a soft-coloured bikini, was standing silently in the hall, listening intently to Clint's conversation.

"Give me thirty minutes, then go. For Christ's sake, don't prolong the entry, don't give them a reason to become suspicious," he said, hanging up the phone as Karen moved quietly to his side.

"Can I be of help?" she offered.

"You've already done enough. Now it's our turn," replied Clint, holding her firmly but gently with both hands.

"How's everything going?" asked Bill, moving next to Karen then looking at Clint, knowing the time was close. "Is it time?"

"It's time!" replied Clint now joined by Peta, still dripping water on the floor from her swim with Saara. Peta's eyes were asking the question.

"Look after my man," she said softly, holding Clint firmly by the hand.

"Don't worry," he answered, gently squeezing.

"I'm coming with you!" said Bill, hurrying after Clint.

"No!" came the reply, then he said, "Perhaps you could be useful," as they both disappeared quickly out the doors, Peta and Karen following them down the stairs with their eyes.

The sting was simple. Using the old house in the suburbs partially owned by the magazine and now unoccupied, they set up a link direct to the Central Computer. Hopefully Ramos, Prodi or whoever lurked in the shadows, would investigate the entry into the computer, checking out the new location, thus enabling Clint and Dusty to back trace their movements and discover some identities and with any luck, their whereabouts.

Chapter 31

Bill could clearly see the expectation on Clint's face. Here was a man living on the edge, though gentle, excitement was his reason for being.

The silence in the car, together with the cold stare in Clint's eyes creating a sense of guilt Bill had not witnessed before. He felt strangely good as both calmness and nervousness clearly showed in his mood, a mood growing with each passing moment of expectation.

Clint reversed the car into the driveway of the vacant house opposite. The owner of the house was busy travelling overseas. He had asked Howard to keep an eye on the property for him while he was away so using the drive was no problem. The windows of his car were heavily tinted, allowing them to see out, but no one in. Only the music from the car radio cut through the tension

They sat watching the street for what seemed an eternity, their conversation barely rising above trivia as Bill's mind drifted slowly to the canyons of Arizona, reliving the short time he'd spent with the Apache people.

Suddenly Clint shocked him back to reality. The blue Ford had stopped opposite and without warning the windows of the house started exploding, glass and wood splintering into oblivion. The only tell-tale signs as to what was happening were tiny puffs of smoke coming from the open back window of the Ford. Clint opened the door to the sound of metal tearing as his bullets found their mark, ripping into the side of the Ford. But with everyone using silencers, the difficulty was detecting where the shots were coming from. Bill sat nervously in the passenger seat observing the shootings, when the windshield of Clint's car exploded, spraying glass throughout the car with lead slashing heavily into the seats.

"Christ!" he yelled, flinging his person to the safety of the floor with the shots continuing, bullets piercing closed doors lodged in the dash, but the radio, undaunted, played the love songs of a past era, the Beatles thumping out the tune, 'Love, Love Me Do'.

As quickly as it had begun all became quiet, but not before Clint's car had received extensive damage. Holes riddled the hood and not a window was still whole. Bill mustered up the courage to look through the missing windshield, at the same time Dusty who had joined Clint opened the door of the Ford. The listless body of the driver slumped over the wheel slid lifelessly to the pavement.

"Dusty! What's wrong with these assholes?" Bill heard Clint say.

"They're trigger happy," replied Dusty, shaking his head in disbelief at the useless waste of life. "These two young people. They're not the ones I expected and positively not FBI."

"Look at the old fart!" said Clint. "That's Peter Savage!"

"Peter Savage, the bastard they couldn't pension off?" asked Dusty.

"Yes. He was J. Edgar's right hand man way back when. He is or was absolutely FBI," said Clint. "I don't understand. No one had to die. At least not today! This was not supposed to happen. Three bodies here and not a clue as to whom had sent them, or where they were coming from!"

When Clint returned to the car, Bill noticed blood trickling from his left hand, the arm hanging limply from his side.

"Let's get out of here," he said, sliding into the passenger seat next to Bill, not bothering to brush away the broken glass. "Back to the station! Dusty and Mick will be following." There was no visible sign of pain on his face.

"What about your arm?" asked Bill, concerned as the blood was now flowing freely.

"It's right!" Clint replied, adding pressure to the blood-soaked area beneath the coat.

Bill started the engine but barely recognized the once mighty V8. The noises emanating from beneath the hood were evidence that major damage had been sustained. Holes riddling the bonnet poured jets of steam towards the missing windshield as Bill drove nervously back to the station.

* * *

Arriving at KWB and finding the security gates open they quickly moved to the underground car park pulling into Hamish's private space with Shelly, personal secretary to Hamish greeting them by the lift.

"Are you all right, sir?" she asked Clint cautiously, closing the door to the lift behind them.

"Yes thank you! Only a scratch," replied Clint with the doors opening to Hamish's office.

"I'll get you a compress!" she said, immediately leaving the room with Hamish moving to greet them.

"What went wrong?" asked Hamish highly concerned at Clint's blood-soaked coat.

"Somehow they knew we were there and were ready for us," replied Dusty.

"Ready? How could they be ready?" asked Hamish.

"I wish I knew. There has to be a bug somewhere!" said Clint.

"There can't be! Mick's been over the entire house!" replied Hamish, standing beside him looking down on the street. "Mick's searched every nook and cranny. He found nothing!"

"Then what's the answer?" asked Dusty as Shelly entering the office carrying a first aid kit. "There has to be something somewhere that we missed. It can't be coincidence. Not all these times!"

Shelly gently removed the coat, taking great care not to further open the wound. Ripping off the shirt sleeve she placed a cold compress bandage to the damaged area, strapping his arm firmly to his waist.

"How the hell is a man gonna take a leak wrapped like this?" asked Clint forcefully.

"With extreme difficulty, I should think," she replied, smiling sweetly. "But a woman can quickly change things with the stroke of a hand."

As her words hit home Clint found it hard to swallow, his dark complexion hiding the redness on his face. He was blushing as a kid in school but couldn't do a thing about it. He felt embarrassed by her words but exhilarated by her thoughts.

"Sorry to interrupt you two! But who were they?" asked Hamish with Dusty rising slowly from the lounge and moving to where Hamish and Clint stood.

"The old man, he was Peter Savage, J. Edgar's closest informer," replied Clint.

"So we're still dealing with the people from the past?" asked Hamish.

"Absolutely," said Clint.

"Personally I'm glad he's gone. I swear he was the bastard with Prodi when Cathryn supposedly jumped to her death!" said Hamish, a smile on his face but sadness in his eyes as he moved back to his desk, lighting himself a cigar.

"The young ones! They're trouble," said Dusty throwing two wallets on Hamish's desk

"How so?" inquired Hamish.

"Does the name Damien Luichi ring a bell?" asked Clint.

"He wouldn't by chance be related to Giuseppi?" asked Hamish.

"I'm afraid so. Nephew," replied Dusty.

"How the hell did he get involved?" asked Hamish, leaning back in his plush leather chair, now puffing heavily on the cigar.

"All this shit dates directly back to J. Edgar!" said Dusty. "And the people we are now dealing with are not amused when someone related gets wasted."

Shelly, not bothering to knock once again entered the office and stood waiting patiently at Hamish's desk, her eyes looking quietly at the man.

"Yes, Shelly?" said Hamish.

"Shall I serve lunch?" A smile filled her well-tanned face as earlier she had caught Mick's glance eyeing her shapely legs.

"Thanks! That would be nice," replied Hamish.

She turned and left, with all eyes following her closely to the door.

"Please, Dusty, continue," said Hamish, partially apologizing for Shelly's interruption.

"Giuseppi Luichi Givarni was once one of Hoover's puppets!" continued Dusty, turning to face Clint. "Hoover's private files supposedly contained questionable evidence of Giuseppi's operations as head of the Mafia. He used those files in the Sixties and Seventies for his own purposes to control the Mafia and in turn help do his bidding."

"Go on," said Clint as some of these revelations were new to him and he really needed to know the truth.

"I believe that's why the young ones died. Damien died because the old man still thinks the FBI has his file and he used the young ones to do his bidding," said Dusty.

"Is there such a file?" asked Hamish, looking directly at Clint.

"Not that I'm familiar with. But only J. Edgar himself could answer that question!" replied Clint glancing over at Dusty and shrugging his shoulders.

"Doesn't make sense," replied Hamish.

"But it does," retorted Dusty. "Hoover had the best of both worlds at his beck and call. The word was when Kennedy was assassinated, the Mafia, along with the FBI were responsible. The Mafia fired from the knoll while Hoover's men framed Lee Harvey. Now the old man believes Ramos has acquired the files."

"I see where you're heading," said Hamish. "I'll personally contact Giuseppi and enlighten him as to our beliefs, and apologize for his loss. Hopefully that will stop further bloodshed! He still wields the axe."

Shelly re-entered the office, placing a tray of sandwiches on the small table in the corner of the room.

Glancing at the faces around the office, Dusty could see she held a captive audience.

"Coffee won't be long," she said smiling knowing it was the furthest thing from anyone's mind.

"Shelly, please!" requested Hamish.

"Sorry, Sir," she replied, smiling and winking at Mick as he responded with a wave.

"Would it be all right to leave Clint's car in the bottom garage?" asked Dusty.

"Why?" replied Hamish, partly confused at the request.

"It requires some minor repairs," said Dusty, smiling partially as everyone moved slowly to the lift.

"Anything I can do?" asked Hamish.

"No! I'll have someone collect it in the morning," replied Clint. "But thanks for the offer."

The door to the office closed as the lift started down.

Chapter 32

The following morning, Bill seated on the balcony overlooking the pool and trying to piece together the story on the virus so far was joined by Mick, two cold beers in hand.

"What are you doing?" Mick asked, observing the girls sunbaking beside the pool while catching up on the local gossip.

"Mick, this isn't what I wanted to write about," said Bill, his eyes fixed on the paper.

"Bill, there are people out there who deserve the truth!"

"I can appreciate that. But how do you tell it? How do you tell people that HIV/AIDS is a man-made virus, a virus created by a brutal but trusted government body? How do you tell a mother her unborn baby is dying from AIDS? How do you apologize to the people affected, not directly, but the loved ones left to wonder what might have been? The innocent ones who haven't lived? How do you tell them that a government body needed to control the homosexual and as such we needed AIDS? It's all too fucked," said Bill, his voice becoming increasingly angry.

"I don't know Bill. But don't let your emotions control your pen. Tell it like it is," said Mick, sipping slowly from his long cold beer while waving to the girls directly beneath him. "Have you ever walked the Wall of Faces?" he said.

"No, I haven't," replied Bill.

"Walk the Walk. Then you and Linda write your story," said Mick then moved closer to where Clint and Dusty were locked in a fiercely contested game of chess.

Bill pondered carefully the words Mick had spoken. One part of him wanted desperately to write the truth, his other part felt the shame the homosexual had had to bear and the ridicule he'd put up with through no fault of his own, since the inception of AIDS. Either way, the story would surely rock the foundations of America, changing forever the way people in power controlled their office.

"Bill!" yelled Linda, bringing him abruptly back to the now world. "Come and join us!"

"Perhaps later. I really must collect my thoughts," he replied waving with his left hand as the ever present sunshine splashed its rays warmly on his face.

* * *

Hours passed and dinner was all but a forgotten memory. Nathan and Saara had departed early to bed, the others grouped in pairs talking quietly before the open fire, the warm glow from the flames forming delicate tiny figures dancing delightfully on the walls in tune with music playing softly from the radio. Linda and Peta, dressed in silky pyjamas, were snuggled closely together on the plush polar bear rug placed before the fire, laughing and giggling, sipping French champagne while telling male-related jokes.

Clint and Dusty had continued the game of chess started earlier that afternoon. Only the sound of the dogs barking at the moon broke the silence. Mick and Karen were seated close on the lounge when the phone broke the tranquillity.

"Allan! Rather late to be ringing. Something wrong?" asked Dusty with the hour fast approaching midnight.

"Sorry! Only ringing to confirm tomorrow," crackled the voice from the speaker. "Six thirty all right?"

"Six thirty will be fine," replied Dusty, hanging up the receiver.

"What was that all about?" asked Linda, looking delightful as the glow of the fire reflected warmly on her face.

"Allan will be here early tomorrow, at my request. He needs to confer with all of us about the film that was given to Robert Muller," said Dusty.

"Who the hell is Allan?" asked Linda.

"Allan Carter is Robert Mullers boss," replied Clint.

"In that case, I'm off to bed," said Linda, standing slowly, the silk pyjamas hugging closely the curves of her body.

"Likewise," said Peta, folding her hand gently into Dusty's then following Linda out of the room, leaving Clint alone staring at the board.

I adore the rear view of silk pyjamas, especially when they cling, Clint thought to himself as he turned down the lights, and he too headed for bed.

Chapter 33

The light of day peeked through the blinds as Bill moved to the window, puzzled by the sound of cars moving slowly along the driveway, the noise of tiny pebbles shifting beneath the weight of the approaching vehicles. Four black limousines had stopped where Clint, Dusty, Saara and Nathan waited patiently, directly beneath the marble staircase. Doors opened as people moved swiftly to cover the lead car. Moments passed, then out stepped a small dark figure, not the same person who had collected the tiny spool earlier.

From his window Bill couldn't hear their conversation, but from a distance the gestures seemed friendly. He hurriedly moved downstairs to where Mick and the girls waited inside the expensive double glass doors. Hamish, who arrived much earlier, stood outside on the marble landing as Allan and Clint mounted the final step.

Saara and Nathan followed closely, flanked by agents wearing the standard issue mirrored sunglasses, but keeping their distance, with Dusty bringing up the rear.

"Hamish! We meet at last. I've long been an admirer of the way you published your paper in the old days," said the small dark figure, his hand outstretched in friendship.

"Well, thank you," replied Hamish, returning the compliment, partially humbled by the recognition. "I too have enormous respect for the way you turned the Bureau into the open office of today."

"How so?" asked the other, a reassuring smile firmly on his face, removing the sunglasses and his heavy trench coat.

"I still remember the old days of the Firm, secretive and accountable to no one. Hence the problem we have today," said Hamish

"We still have secrets. Especially where national security is concerned, and that's why I'm here," the visitor replied, with everyone moving slowly inside.

With the introductions over, Hamish asked Allan for the reason for the visit, and why he had been called. "Have you seen the film?" he asked.

"Yes!" came the reply. "In private. Then again with the President!"

"The President!" replied Linda in surprise. "As in the United States?"

"Yes. I've kept him informed as to your beliefs."

"And what are his thoughts?" replied Linda, but Allan didn't answer.

"This is not to be swept under the carpet," said Hamish angrily. "Or be filed away by a protective bureaucratic system."

But again Allan didn't reply. He stood in silence observing the faces in the room.

"Mr Carter! Please tell him he's wrong," pleaded Linda.

"The President wants a meeting!" replied Allan.

"When!" replied Linda

"Soon as possible," he replied. "When it suits you!"

"To resolve the matter or to treat it as though nothing happened?" said Linda, staring at Allan in disbelief.

"That I can't answer," replied the small man

"And what of the bastards responsible? Do they just walk?" she said.

"Linda. May I call you that?"

"It's my name!" she replied angrily.

"I don't have a directive. Clint knows the rules. I need presidential intervention to act!"

"Then why hasn't he given it?" she replied, her tone slowly calming.

"It's not that simple," he said, looking to Clint for help.

"Allan is right," said Clint. "His hands are tied!"

"Well, if that's the case, we'll just have to go and see what the White House has to offer," said Dusty.

"Are you happy to come to Washington for the meeting?" asked Allan, showing surprise.

"Conditions will most certainly apply! And why not? Nothing ventured nothing gained," replied Dusty as Saara entered the room, carrying a tray of light refreshments.

"When do we leave?" asked Linda, her anger still evident.

"Not until we have the pages decoded," replied Dusty.

"Can I be of help?" asked Allan, sincerity in his voice and feeling he needed to get back on Linda's good side.

"Not unless you can find Nathan's great great grandfather and somehow get him here," replied Hamish, easing some of the tension that had been steadily building around them.

"Why do you need his grandfather? Has he something to do with the film?" asked Allan, sipping the coffee Saara had prepared.

"To complete the story, we need the old Indian," replied Dusty.

"Nathan thinks the writings are those of the ancient Navaho. The Anasazi," said Mick, desperately trying to enter the conversation.

"And you think the old man can read the encrypted code?" asked Allan.

"Correct," replied Dusty, each taking turns at answering Allan questions.   "The writings may even contain the antidote for HIV."

"That would be handy!" replied Allan.   "How hard have you tried to unravel the code?"

"Mick's tried everything! So far, nothing has even come close to giving up the secret of the pages," replied Dusty, with Linda and the others listened intently.

"Has my office been informed? After all, we have the world's smartest computer."

"I used your computer," replied Mick. "I turned it back on itself. I asked the difficult questions!"

"And?" asked Allan.

"Within minutes, all systems negated. A complete shutdown possibly programmed by Carlo, if he was the one who originally entered the code!" said Mick.

"So that was you!" asked Allan.

"Sorry! But I needed to know," said Mick.

"I see! In that case, could I borrow Nathan's services?"

"You won't find grandfather without me," replied Nathan politely.

"Then by all means, let's make haste!" smiled Allan for he finally had something to smile about, a smile that came hard to his face.

Chapter 34

The next few days passed slowly and with no word from Allan or Nathan, they needed to escape the house. Linda thought it fitting to pay their respects to those struck down by this deadliest of viruses. The Wall of Faces had been constructed in the mid-eighties by those touched by the virus to remember and honour the AIDS dead. At first, only the sick from the Bay area were honoured, but with the years passing and the toll growing, mourners from around the world joined the parade. Faces stared out from this silent shrine remembering those unlucky enough to have contracted this unforgiving virus. Faces of all ages and nationalities confronted the public who came to mourn the stricken.

They lunched at the small French café bordering the "Wall" before setting off on their walk. Dusty and Peta walked slowly arm in arm, followed closely by Linda and Bill. The day with only a hint of a breeze was warmed gently by the sun. The Wall was constructed to a height of about six feet, and then divided into one foot squares, each representing the window of a dear departed. Some had pictures, some with candles, but each contained the memory of a loved one. The shrine honoured the homosexual, bisexual, transsexual, heterosexual, haemophiliac, the young and the innocent, each remembered in a special way. For almost two hours they walked the wall, the dead numbering in the thousands, a list growing daily. Young faces staring out from windowed prisons reflecting their plight. If one stopped to listen, you could almost hear the muffled cries seeping from the cold, cold caverns of the Wall. Loved ones from all religions knelt and prayed, crying unashamedly while making peace with their God. Linda stopped and knelt down beside the picture of a beautiful young boy, the inscription beneath his photo read simply,

"Dear God, take pity. He has not asked for, but received."
"Not the gift of life! But a legacy of man!"
He was aged only nine.

Linda, rising from her knees, turned to Bill bursting into tears.

"What have we done?" she cried with Bill embracing her tenderly, trying to comfort her as she could no longer bear the pain and sorrow attached to the Wall, her emotions shattered and wanting to leave this place of remembrance immediately.

"Darling I feel the same. I feel the shame," he replied in anger with tears also forming in his eyes. "I feel the sorrow. But utmost I now feel the compulsion to write the truth. I now know what we need to write. We must somehow help release their souls to their God. And for Christ's sake, let mankind know what we have done!"

At first his words didn't mean much to her, but later that day helped fill the empty void she was experiencing deep within herself.

* * *

Returning home to a hot afternoon, they found their relaxation and solitude by the pool and were soon joined by Saara in her familiar bikini.

"I now know what we need to write," said Bill. The sight of the Wall still burnt deep in his mind.

"About what?" asked Peta in her soft voice.

"The Virus! The truth! The whole truth! And nothing but the truth! The disturbing injustice we have created," replied Bill, with a serious, unfamiliar tone, creeping into his voice.

"Any word from Nathan?" Linda asked Saara in a hushed tone.

"Do we know an ETA?" she said cautiously while splashing her toes briskly in the water.

"Yes! He and Mick spoke earlier. I believe he's on the way home," she replied, her figure tight and firm had droplets of water dripping delicately from her chin. They were soon joined by Mick holding on tight to Saara, fearing retaliation for the fact that he had earlier unsuspectingly and with great pleasure, pushed her into the deep end of the pool.

"Mick any idea when they are due back?" continued Linda, as the sound of an approaching helicopter thumped loudly.

"No idea," yelled Mick as the noise from the distance became almost deafening.

A gunship appeared from behind the house hovering over the open lawns, with the water in the pool whipped to a frenzied lather by the power of the blades. Things began to fall silent as the helicopter landed and the powerful rotors stopped spinning. The doors of the gunship opened slowly, with two armed Marines moving swiftly to the grass. They were followed closely by Allan and Nathan standing in the doorway, helping the old Indian to the ground. The women by the pool in awe of the power of the gunship waved their message to the delight of the marines. Dusty moved quickly to where Allan waited, hugging Nathan in the process as Clint nodded approval from the balcony.

"You did it!" said Dusty.

"You doubted me?" replied Allan.

"I'm a realist," answered Dusty, acknowledging the Marines with a salute.

"Then answer me this! When we landed in the Valley of Ten Thousand Smokes, the old man was waiting. How did he know we were coming?" asked Allan.

"How could he?" replied Dusty. "Nathan must have contacted him!"

"He says not!" answered Allan.

"I don't know the answer, but I'm delighted we have him!" replied Dusty.

"Strange," said Allan a bewildered look on his face. "Anyway, I'll see you soon," he continued. The noise started again as the helicopter lifted then disappeared into the distance, beneath the Golden Gate overlooking San Francisco with naval vessels scattered around the Bay.

The Chief, a small man, had history etched deep into his face. His hair was pulled tight and beaded into pigtails. He looked in astonishment at the size and colour of Clint who had joined them with his hand outstretched in friendship. The pale denim shirt blended favourably with his Levies and the moccasins completed the picture. Before them stood the past!

"History has not been kind to your people," said Clint.

"Not history! The greed of the white man," the Chief replied slowly in his Indian accent. "Your people too have suffered," the old man said, moving with Mick to the balcony overlooking the pool.

"Chief, I don't mean to rush you, but can you read this?" asked Mick, placing the pages before him.

The old Indian paused, looking closely at the writings.

"These are the words of the Old Ones! It will take time," he replied, as the girls by the pool were again joined by Nathan. The old Indian glanced at the pages, his eyes occasionally crossing the table towards Mick, Karen remaining close by his side.

"These pages I will do tonight! I wish not to continue at the moment," he said, to Mick's surprise.

"I understand! You must be tired," replied Mick.

"Not so, young master! I feel the aura of past and present around us, never a good sign," he said, moving leisurely inside with Karen in close pursuit, carrying his only bag.

"What did you make of that?" asked Dusty.

"Daunting!" replied Clint shaking his head in disbelief.

*   *   *

Midnight and the lights from the candles flickered boldly from the old man's room. Incense drifted thick on the air as he chanted incantations, calling for the Old Ones to help unravel these most ancients of writings. Shadows filled the room as the pages unfolded.

Nathan sat listening quietly in the comfort of the bay window, his knees tucked tightly beneath his chin as he stared into the darkness. Saara was fast asleep in the top bunk unaware of the pain the old Indian was going through. The writings hadn't come easy, and as the story unfolded the chanting became louder. By dawn they could be heard throughout the house.

Chapter 35

Clint and Dusty, the only ones dressed, moved slowly to the kitchen with the fire in the main room long since cold. The girls in pyjamas joined them soon after. Dusty prepared the coffee while awaiting the arrival of the Chief. Saara joined them late, for she had slept too well. The noise of the night had bothered all but her and she felt refreshed and showed it in her complexion.

"Saara, how did grandfather go last night?" asked Dusty as Nathan joined them at the opposite end of the table.

"I don't know! When I woke the room was empty," she replied softly, a half-yawn still on her mouth.

"Grandfather and the Humans did as Mick asked," said Nathan, pouring himself a glass of cold milk from the jug placed earlier on the table by Dusty.

"Humans?" asked Dusty, as Mick hurriedly entered the kitchen, followed closely by Karen.

"Exactly what do you mean when you say the "Humans?" said Clint quietly, his arm supporting his head. He held a cup of coffee in hand and tried desperately not to show the pain of a hangover.

"The chanting is only ever used when a race of people cease to exist!" replied Nathan with the horror of sadness deep in his eyes.

"How so?" asked Linda, sitting balanced on the stool, her feet tucked delicately beneath her.

"I'm not really sure! He used the ancient words. Words I'm not familiar with," replied Nathan reluctantly.

"I don't follow," replied Linda, now stretching her legs from under her torso.

"The Ancient Ones described themselves as human beings. The beholders of life," answered Nathan. "They valued greatly the essence of the spirit within. And above all, respect for each other."

"How does this involve the writings?" said Peta who was unfamiliar with the ways of the American Indian.

"The Chief will reveal all in good time," replied Nathan.

As Karen was placing a light breakfast on the dining table, the room fell suddenly silent for in the door stood the old Indian dressed in the traditional buckskins with the war paint etched deep onto his face. The headdress of eagle feathers stretched to the floor and in his hand he held the pages.

"Chief, what's wrong?" asked Linda, realizing he looked in pain, but he didn't answer, choosing to stand in silence.

"Your people never stop! First you eliminate the Human Beings. Now you eradicate yourselves! Why?" he said, staring coldly into the quiet room.

"Chief, what have you found?" asked Peta politely, her voice soft but sure.

The Chief moved slowly to the table, studying the faces around him. Slowly in his own unique way he started to answer Peta's question.

"Only after the last tree has been felled.

Only after the last river has been poisoned.

Only after the last fish has perished.

Only then will you find, it's all too late!"

He moved closer to the table placing the pages in front of Mick. "Read, so all may hear," he said, looking slowly around the room.

"That won't be possible," said Karen softly. "I need the pages. If you would be so kind, nobody need get hurt," she said, holding a deadly .38 snub nose gun tightly in one hand, the other extended towards Mick, ready to receive the pages.

"Put the gun down," said Clint in his firm voice, standing directly behind her by the fireplace.

She heard his demand, but in the same instant turned and squeezed off two shots, The first one shattering the vase on the mantle, the other hitting Clint in the chest. Almost simultaneously Clint's gun fired. It was a powerful magnum, hitting Karen under the right breast, the force hurling her body across the room and with a sickening thud slammed against the glass door leading to the kitchen.

Ears rang in pain; the stench of gunpowder overwhelmed them, splattered bloodstains covering the pastel walls. Peta and Linda had crouched down behind the main table, the suddenness of the moment taking all by surprise. Dusty moved quickly to Clint's aid, the big man was sitting holding his chest. Bill followed as quickly as his legs allowed expecting to find Clint covered in blood. Instead he sat rubbing his chest forcefully, cursing himself for not reacting quicker.

"Damn fine issues, these vests! Still hurts like shit," Clint said with Dusty and Bill helping him off the floor and moving to where Karen lay, face down in a pool of blood mixed with the broken glass from the lead lined door. Clint gently sat her up trying not to further hurt her, but being in shock she felt no pain.

"Why?" asked Clint, the sadness deep in his eyes.

"For mum," she replied, the blood gurgling thick at the back of her throat.

"You threatened to expose names after all these years, to tell an unsuspecting world of things they have no right to know."

"Karen! This makes no sense," whispered Clint softly. "We've already viewed the film. We know the truth."

"Yes! But the pages would confirm it. The film can be explained away. But not so the writings!" she replied, her voice fading slowly.

"You didn't have to die! Not today! Not like this," said Dusty, glancing over Clint's shoulder at the blood-soaked body he held in his arms.

"I believe in what has happened. I believe in the cause, as I believed in the occasion when they rid the country of Kennedy."

Clint's eyes lit up, jerking her forward, a grimace of pain appearing on her face as she let out a scream.

"Who had Kennedy killed?" shouted Clint, trying desperately to reach her fading spirit.

"Why, Karen? Why did they release the virus?" asked Bill softly, kneeling beside her.

"Dear Bill!" she replied, looking up at him, the pain on her face slowly fading. "Man must stop his promiscuous ways. Can't you see? This is the perfect solution, rid the world of homosexuals and keep everyone to one partner!"

"Tell me who ordered Kennedy killed!" demanded Clint, with rage set deep in his eyes.

"Clint! Don't!" pleaded Linda, the tears rolling freely from her eyes.

"Karen, please!" said Clint. "I must know the truth."

"Look to Johnston," whispered Karen. "He wanted what Kennedy had. And the only way to get it was to side with Hoover. Hoover convinced him that Kennedy was destroying the American way and he had to go." She gasped as her body flinched then became limp with her eyes rolling back as her blood-soaked remains sank lifeless to the floor.

"Forty years!" yelled Clint, standing over her body with blood covering his front and hands and tears of anguish streaming down his cheeks. "Now I find I've protected the bastards that rid the country of greatness!" he said, still the tears flowing freely from his dark eyes.

"Forget Kennedy," said Dusty, as Linda hurriedly placed a towel over Karen's body, the blood quickly soaking through, highlighting the sadness of the moment that had just passed.

"Now we know why they were always one step ahead!" said Mick.

"Yes! She was her mother's sleeper. But why would a mother do that to her daughter?" replied Dusty as Linda shook her head in disbelief.

"Did she poison the dogs?" asked Saara, standing silently in her nightdress, glancing sadly at the sad remains.

"Yes! But the poison would not have killed them. It simply immobilized them and I suspect before Ramos could move on us that night, Clint arrived," said Dusty.

The old Indian moved away, looking closely at the fallen body, Mick in close pursuit.

"So this is what you meant by past and present around us," said Mick, saddened by, but keeping his focus on the truth about the events that had just occurred.

"Yes!" the Chief replied. "Her aura was not with you. Such a waste! The way of the white man!"

"This was not started by us, Old Man!" replied Clint.

"No! But your ways have not changed, Older Man."

"She was always sentenced to death by her mother, Older Older Man!"

"Now you see my point Older Older Older Man?" the Chief concluded, a hint of a smile on his lips.

"Why would Victoria Prodi sentence her own daughter to death? And how do you know for sure that Karen was Victoria's daughter?" Mick asked of Clint.

"I last saw Karen at a swim party put on by Ramos and Prodi to celebrate their rise to prominence thirty years ago. I remember she was a beautiful young woman with two tiny doves tattooed on her right side bikini line to cover an appendix scar that threatened to ruin her looks. I felt I recognized her face from the past the first time we met in the hall, but sadly I couldn't place her. It was only when you ladies were sunbaking around the pool the other day I spotted the tattoo then the penny dropped."

"But why sacrifice your own daughter?" repeated Mick.

"They simply couldn't take the chance that 73 might have told Linda something. Something that they didn't want made public," replied Dusty, still wiping the blood from his hands. "The stakes were too high."

"Then really she died for nothing," said Mick, a look of disbelief still on his face.

"Affirmative!" said Clint quietly with a lump deep in his throat, the suddenness of the moment etched deeply on his face. He had killed a woman in self defence but it had made the moment no easier to bear as he had feelings for her and felt she too had feelings for him.

Chapter 36

An hour had passed when the limos reappeared at the gate, the lead car flashing its lights to open the gate.

"What the fuck's happened here?" asked Allan as he moved quickly through the doors, again flanked by his men and cautiously stepping over the broken glass scattered across the floor.

"Same shit! New day," replied Dusty, with Allan stopping by the smashed doors looking at the blood-splattered walls and the frail limp body beneath the blood-soaked towel.

"Jesus Christ! Did you have to use a cannon?" asked Allan Carter.

"Yeah," Clint replied despairingly, looking down at Karen's body.

"Now things make sense. They used a sleeper. Prodi's own daughter," said Allan.

"Damn! This fucking code better be worth it," blasted Clint.

"There wasn't a thing you could have done to prevent what happened," said Linda attempting to comfort the big man.

Clint didn't answer, he liked Karen, and his feelings were confused as only the previous night they had enjoyed each other's company.

"The decoded pages. Can I have them?" asked Allan, with one hand extended.

"When we're finished," replied Clint. "We've come too far to not confirm the truth!"

"But the President's waiting!" replied Allan.

Clint merely looked at Allan as Mick picked up the bloodstained pages moving everyone to the sunroom. In the meantime, the old Indian had packed his belongings and stored them neatly by the door as Mick started to read the pages.

"This entry is my last, for Ramos has ordered six of us to leave for Columbia in the morning, something I don't feel comfortable about. The infighting since the release of the virus keeps everyone apart. Only Savage and Prodi, sometimes Ramos, meet regularly. Antonio Demagos suspects Victoria of injecting him with the plague she calls her own and I feel that unless we do as asked, we will suffer the same fate.

"Prodi of late has become a complete psychopath. Life means nothing to the woman. People who stand in her way simply vanish, never to be heard of again. She's totally committed to J. Edgar's original script of eradicating the homosexual. I feel time running out for surely somebody must soon realize how we mutated a monkey virus then released it on the unsuspecting world.

"I should have guessed things were not right when the four biochemists working at the hospital fell to their deaths while holidaying in Mexico. Mechanical failure of the brakes was blamed for the accident. Then when the last two lab technicians perished in a horrific explosion, the wrong labelling of crucial elements was to blame.

When the Hoover institute was destroyed and burnt to the ground to cover their tracks, the antidote that I suspect never existed also vanished."

Bill looked to Allan, who was listening intently as Mick read the pages, shaking his head in disbelief as Mick continued.

"The virus was first released into Zaire, Central Africa in 1970 to test the effect of the virus and the strength of the antidote. The results we discovered all too late. Within weeks somehow the antitoxins used as the antidote caused the virus to mutate within itself killing the entire village. Two hundred and seventy-four people perished within a month of us injecting the virus antidote. We had created Ebola!

"And again it was much too late, as the originally released virus had rapidly spread throughout the country. A truth we later found out when we returned.

"I truly regret having a hand in the release of the virus into Africa and if anyone ever asked the source of the virus they would automatically look to central Africa as the starting point of the HIV virus."

Mick stopped reading.

The old Indian had heard enough. He picked up his belongings and quietly disappeared out the door.

"Chief where are you going?" asked Dusty, following him to the marble stairs outside.

"I have much unfinished business," the Chief replied, his bag hanging loosely over his shoulder. "The wise ones await me!"

"Can I give you a lift?" asked Dusty.

"No, what I do, I must do alone."

"Would you let Nathan go with you?"

"He cannot yet travel on the spiritual plane," said the old Indian.

This didn't make any sense to Dusty, but he respected the old man's ways and reluctantly bent to his wishes.

"Then remain close to the Great Spirit," said Dusty, as the old Indian now dressed in moccasins and denim moved quietly out of sight.

"Where is he going?" asked Clint, joining Dusty at the head of the stairs.

"He didn't say!" replied Dusty. The tranquillity offered by the Chief was now gone.

"Where do you suppose he'd go?" said Dusty, looking closely at the trodden path the old man had taken.

"He knows what he has to do," replied Clint, moving back inside.

Mick took up the pages and began reading again.

"Six months later in September of 1970, we first released the virus on American soil in San Francisco. Then six months later we repeated the exercise in New York At first we thought we'd failed. Then in '72 Hoover died suddenly in office leaving Ramos in charge. He and Prodi took full control and with friends in high places, how high I never learned, but they had no one to answer to. We all went on with business as usual as there were no recorded deaths or any sign of illness amongst the homosexual sector for what seemed an eternity. Then one day in late '74, a small article appeared in the New York Times describing the unusual deaths of three active homosexuals. Somehow their immune systems had comprehensively broken down, causing death from complications. Doctors at the Centre for Disease Control were convinced the new virus was airborne, so the strain

continued unchecked for a further eighteen months. Not until Terrance Higgins died in England in 1980 did things start to become clear. Thank God a young lab assistant accidentally discovered traces of a new virus in the blood during a routine autopsy. However, it took twelve months to convince her seniors that the strain was body fluid related. The different laboratories around the world had all isolated the new strain but did not listen to the obvious and so it went unchecked for a further eighteen months.

"These were absolutely the best eighteen months of Victoria's life. She'd ring and laugh at the attempts made by the medical profession to find the cause. The last few years have taken their toll, now women and children are dying from related symptoms. Victoria moved quickly to convince the American people through the American Medical Society that the new virus was homosexually manifested and with the evidence and ignorance of the day, became the accepted solution. They also put forward a second theory in case the first was asked.

"The second theory involved the chimpanzees of the Congo carrying the virus, with the local aborigines killing the monkeys for their meat. They, the experts blame the mixing of the blood during the slaughter of the apes for the creation of the virus. What a load of crap. If anyone believes that, then Santa Claus lives.

There exists a microfilm showing technicians now dead, along with the English professor Farnsworth killed by Ramos and Prodi, changing the virus bacterially using human genes and chromosomes injected directly into the monkey strain. I know that hundreds of homosexuals were used as guinea pigs during the early years of experimentation at the Hoover institute, none ever released for all were killed and their bodies incinerated. The incinerator was fired up every night after midnight to rid us of the experimental bodies and also to conceal our tracks. On their foreheads were tattooed the day, month and year each had been injected with the experimental virus. Everyone working at the hospital cleaners, nurses, doctors all met with some form of fatal accident each investigated by the FBI, a considerable joke back then. I placed this code deep inside the central computer for Ramos knew the film existed and if something went wrong, hopefully someone in search of the truth would discover my message. God help us all.

"I'm still amazed that that world hasn't launched a complete and honest investigation into the real cause of the HIV virus. First we blamed the homosexuals. Then we blamed the chimps of the Congo. I beg and challenge anyone who reads my message to question the norm. Homosexuality has been occurring for centuries and nothing changed yet when we discover how to genetically and bacterially manipulate the genes and chromosomes, we have AIDS. To cure the man-made virus is only possible by first understanding the monkey version. Then trace that version back to the source, the original beginnings. Cure the monkey version and you cure the human strain.

"I trusted no one with the key to the code except my younger sister Peta. I gave her a small box to hold a key. The key along with the clipping will show the way!

"Don't trust the White House. The Admiral, whose name I'm not familiar with, along with a certain General are now in complete control. The President I think knows, but so far has done nothing to punish those responsible *and seems lost to the seriousness of the moment. Hopefully -*

There, the message ended. The mood in the room had turned sombre, for now they understood the old Indian's pain.

"You cannot take this seriously," said Allan quietly.

"If Nixon and Regan knew, then how many others at the Oval Office are involved?" replied Dusty, his voice partly disguising his anger.

"I don't believe the Oval office is involved. Not according to my sources. Besides we have a meeting with the President," said Allan.

"We?" asked Clint, standing at the window staring at the view across the chasms with the lavishly built mansions dotting the hillside.

"Yes! He's studied the film at length and wishes to offer a form of retribution," replied Allan.

"To us for finding the truth, or those touched by the virus?" asked Linda angrily.

"I'll let the President answer all your questions."

"I'm not sure that that's a good idea," replied Dusty, standing beside Clint, observing the faces around the room.

"I have a bad feeling about this one. Call it a hunch," Dusty said.

"Why are you looking at me? I'll do everything in my power to help any way I can, short of treason," said Allan, looking back at the faces around him.

"What about it, Dusty?" asked Linda. "The only way of getting the truth out, is to go!"

"You could be right. But I don't feel good about it," Dusty replied reluctantly looking to Clint for confirmation.

"I'll get busy cleaning up this mess," said Peta.

"Please, don't bother," replied Allan. "My people will take care of everything!"

"What's going to become of Karen's body?" asked Peta.

"Like all traitors, she'll be buried in a pauper's grave," replied Allan.

"Can't you do better than that?" asked Clint. "Even though she was Prodie's daughter and worse, a sleeper I still feel we owe her something!"

"I can't even begin to imagine how you all felt towards Karen. But I'll do everything in my power to see that she has a proper Christian burial!" replied Allan looking now at Peta for a comforting reply.

"Thank you," replied Peta gratefully, then Allan walked back to the awaiting cars.

Chapter 37

The sun was just rising as the Airforce helicopter landed on the lawns of the house. Marines stood by the steps leading to the helicopter awaiting their departure to the airport. The short flight was made thrilling beyond measure as the young pilot skimmed the rooftops then thundered down valleys, slicing between housing and lifting suddenly high into the cool crisp morning sky. A quick pass under the Gate, then on to the airport, landing beside a Gulfstream executive jet, waiting in a private section of the airport. They no sooner had boarded than the twin engines roared into action and the Gulfstream thundered down the runway and into the air.

"Military VIP flight," said Mick to nobody in particular as they climbed into the pure blue sky.

"I was hoping for Airforce One," said Mick.

"Not a chance," replied Clint. "For a start, that plane is only used for presidential flights and anyway, it would attract too much attention."

The flight to Washington had gone smoothly, two young women working as flight attendants and ensured the trip was a pleasant one with free-flowing drinks and a meal that would have put to shame even a first-class cabin dinner in a commercial airliner.

* * *

On landing, they were directly transferred to another helicopter for the trip to the Oval Office. The flight took no time and soon they landed on the White House lawns, met by the President's personal bodyguard, a close associate of Clint's.

"The President will meet with you in the morning," said the short stocky figure standing before them. "He's sorry and sends his regards but urgent meetings of national security need his full attention. If you would care to follow me, I'll show you to your quarters. You know how it is," he said, looking to Clint for confirmation.

"He's playing golf, isn't he?" replied Clint.

"Now I know why you're the best! Yes he is."

Clint only nodded then followed the others inside.

The Presidential suite had only recently been redecorated, painted a soft white. The smell of fresh paint lingered heavily in the air and it came as a wondrous relief when the maids who were stationed outside their room, opened the large bay windows leading to the balcony overlooking the lawns. Fresh air rolling in replaced the closeness and the aroma of turpentine hanging thick in the rooms. All the ceilings were extremely high domed laden with expensive chandeliers, spinning the colours of the rainbow delicately across the marbled floors' then dancing up the walls. The rooms throughout the White House displayed the splendour and the vastness of space offered by the Oval Office.

Portraits of all past Presidents dotted the walls, observing each new resident as they entered their space. Every bedroom, and there were five, possessed uniquely hand-carved four poster beds, king sized and inlaid with white gold etched deeply in early American, to commemorate the passing of the Civil War and the peace between the Union. Dusty, Bill, Mick and Nathan resided in the eastern wing, and commanded the same space and luxury afforded the girls. However the portraits were not those of Presidents, but of their brides, each framed in black and white in keeping with tradition.

"Where are your quarters?" asked Mick, looking at Clint.

"I don't stay at the White House. I have my own apartment in DC."

"But all this luxury," replied Mick.

"It's a worry," said Clint laughingly.

"Let's see what the girls are doing," said Bill, anxious to have a closer look at this wondrous institution.

In their own quarters, the girls were equally impressed.

"What do you think Saara? Isn't it gorgeous?" asked Linda, gesturing at the splendour surrounding them.

"No, Linda," said Saara. "I think this is an expensive waste! People in America living in poverty, and he lives like this."

"But he's the President," replied Linda, partly surprised at her answer, feeling the fine soft leather of the sofa.

"I don't care who he is. He's no better than your average person," Saara replied sharply, moving to the bedroom.

"What's this all that about?" said Linda, turning to Peta.

"She's a proud one. And, judging by her tone, dislikes waste!" replied Peta.

"This is waste?" asked Linda.

"In her eyes, yes," replied Peta.

The knock at the door was answered immediately by the tall slender maid.

"Well, hello," said Mick, looking at the young maid standing beside her friend, both eager to please in any way possible and looking back at Mick. "They treating you ladies all right?" he said, with the tall brunette blushing before she answered.

"Yes, Sir," she replied in a distinct southern drawl.

"You all from the South?" taunted Mick.

"Sure am," she replied, not realizing he was having fun at her expense.

"Would you kindly excuse us?" said Dusty, escorting the young maids to the waiting room directly outside the door. "Mick will be joining you shortly," he said, closing the doors behind them.

"Southern girls in the White House," smiled Linda.

"They fit the décor. Also, it keeps the balance of voters happy," replied Clint.

"Political ploy?" queried Linda.

"Call it what you will! It works," said Clint with a smile.

"I think it's a great idea," said Mick gleefully.

"You would," said Linda, smiling. "Go on, get out of here!"

Mick didn't have to be asked a second time, and quickly moved to join the girls in the outside waiting room. The furnishings here were totally different to those within. The walls contained the portraits of legendary Generals, Colonel Davy Crockett holding centre stage, keeping the balance of power in perspective. On the opposite wall hung the paintings of their nemesis the once mighty Sitting Bull and Crazy Horse, the Indian heroes to the Little Big Horn massacre.

"Where's Bill?" asked Linda, realizing suddenly he was not in the room.

"He decided to take the guided tour," replied Dusty as Saara, towel wrapped tight around her slim well tanned body and drying her hair moved from the bathroom back to the bedroom, before disappearing through the half open door. All eyes followed her movements as she stepped in front of the full-length mirror, drying her hair vigorously. The towel wrapped loosely around her body fell delicately to the floor. Linda, turning to see what was distracting the men, saw that the mirrored image of Saara in full bloom had their undivided attention, she moved quickly to close the door.

"You guys don't miss a trick," she said, waving her finger as Clint and Dusty shrugged their shoulders and looked at each other smiling, but not daring to reply.

Nathan soon joined Mick in the waiting room and together they entertained the young ladies, their laughter echoing long and heavy throughout the hallowed halls, with the eyes of the portraits following them closely as they moved around the room.

Chapter 38

The night passed, and in the morning they found themselves waiting apprehensively in the Oval Office. The American flag, crossed and draped loosely behind the presidential chair, hung proudly alongside the Confederate, a scene that would captured the imagination of whoever entered this sacred office and the silence almost deafening.

Abruptly, the huge doors swing open and they were joined by heavily decorated naval uniforms, each with his own personal secretary, talking at great length amongst themselves, but no one really listening. The President arrived late, surrounded by his personal crowd of self important people. He made his way towards them, shaking hands, acknowledging each individual as he passed, a ritual he performed daily.

"I've heard much about you people," said the President, his hand reaching out to greet them warmly and smiling.

"Ladies and Gentlemen would everyone kindly excuse us and leave the room?" said one of the President's aides in a loud voice. The crowd fell deadly silent with the President himself opening the enormous doors, as Allan, who had arrived earlier, stepped through. The Generals, Admirals and their hangers on, quiet and somewhat confused, moved outside again. Alone at last with the leader of the nation, the most powerful individual on the planet, took his seat behind the enormous desk and looked at Allan to start the conversation.

"We all know why we're here!" began Allan.

"What can I say?" interrupted the President to the sound of the crowd milling restlessly outside the doors. "You have uncovered a horrendous truth. A truly sad truth! However, due to national security, it has now been classified!"

"Classified, Mr. President?" replied Mick, his eyes not leaving those of the President.

"Everything's been done to locate the people responsible. But you must understand the story can never be released. The damage to this office would be catastrophic. America would never recover," said the President in a slow but sure voice.

"In that case, what do you want from us?" asked Linda, looking to Allan with annoyance in her eyes.

"Linda! May I call you that? I need your loyalty, for that I'll make concessions," replied the President, sincerity lying heavy in his voice.

"Yes, you may. And what sort of concessions do you have in mind?" Linda asked.

"Name them!"

"A bribe, Mister President?" queried Linda.

"No. A trade! Nothing said or written can right the wrong that's been committed, but perhaps, hopefully I can make things more bearable," he said.

"Can you bring back the dead? Can you resurrect the young children?" replied Linda, tears forming in her eyes.

"No Linda! That I cannot do. And you ask for my silence. Ask those who have the virus for forgiveness. Ask the families of the now dead. Ask those who in the future will contract the virus. And if they can forgive, then you have my silence. Do you realize that more people have died from AIDS than perished in World Wars One and Two? And we called Hitler a madman!"

Linda's emotions were making it difficult for her to control her voice.

"Mr. President! Could we have time alone?" interrupted Mick, as the stunned silence hung in the room.

"All you need!" replied the President partially relieved at the ending of the conversation he knew he could never win. The President rose from his desk and moved immediately to the outside doors as Allan followed in close pursuit.

"Allan, would you mind remaining?" asked Dusty.

"Mr. President!"

"Please Allan! I'll be outside awaiting some form of an answer!" he replied closing the door as the outside noise once again drifted in filling the room.

"Allan, what's going on?" asked Dusty.

"Absolutely nothing!" replied Allan

"Is he trying to buy our silence?" said Linda.

"No! On the contrary, he's asking things you'd like to see done to help. He's offering unlimited funds in return for your silence and loyalty."

"What about the innocent ones? The ones who have died and those who have for no fault of their own contracted this virus. Don't they have the right?" she said.

"They do! But like he said, it would totally discredit the government. The cost to the taxpayer would amount to countless trillions in ongoing compensation. We simply don't have the money!"

"So we go on letting people believe the virus is homosexually manifested?" replied Linda, disbelief ever present on her face.

"You can do more good with loyalty and resources," said Allan, pacing nervously around the Oval Office.

"I'm not sure I want to be loyal to these people!" replied Mick.

"Not loyal to them. Loyal to your President," answered Allan.

"Could we discuss this further, tonight, amongst ourselves?" asked Mick.

"Mick, he really was hoping to settle the matter today," replied Allan but half not daring to look him in the eye.

"We need more time to get our heads together. We need to discuss the matter in depth," replied Mick, with everyone nodding approval.

"I'll see what I can do," said Allan, opening the doors with the outside office falling totally and completely silent, as all eyes turned in their direction, Allan slowly pushing his way through the crowd, moved to the President's side and quietly whispered his message.

"Not a problem," replied the President, nodding approval over the crowd as the entourage moved back inside the Oval Office with the noise of their conversations starting once again.

"You people take all the time you need! There is no pressure. Hopefully we'll come to a productive conclusion!" yelled the President over the crowd.

"Thank you, Mr. President," replied Linda, closely observing the crowd as they moved hurriedly past.

"I'll be waiting anxiously for your decision! Coming Allan?" said the President

"One moment sir I've a few loose ends to tie up," replied the small man.

"Suit yourself," the President said, closing the doors and silencing the noise once again.

"Are we under threat?" asked Linda, glancing at Allan.

"No, Linda. I'd know if you were."

"Somehow I don't feel comfortable," she replied.

"I think I have the same feeling. A feeling of deceit and deception," said Mick.

"I know these people. They're at odds with what you've uncovered, but they're not stupid," said Allan.

"Can we discuss this further back at the room? All these eyes make me nervous," said Mick, referring to the portraits around the walls.

* * *

"Close the door," said Mick hurriedly, with Peta the last to enter as Mick placed a portable speaker on the table by the window.

"You bugged the Oval Office! Christ, that's treason!" said Allan in a half whisper.

"Allan, you're here because Clint said you were OK, so please," replied Mick, with Allan shaking his head in disbelief, looking over at Clint who was standing next to Dusty as Mick turned up the volume.

"Mr. President! Could General North and myself discuss a delicate matter with you in private?" crackled over the speaker.

"What's this? The day of secrets?" came the reply from the president.

"It's important," said the Admiral.

"Gentlemen, Ladies. You heard Admiral Rasmussen. Would you kindly excuse us once more?" Again the room became alive as the group moved slowly outside, their noise decreasing as they left.

"Rasmussen! Wasn't that the name at the hospital when 73 was moved into isolation?" asked Bill, looking at Linda to confirm his suspicions.

"Mr. President, please be seated," came over the speaker.

"I'm fine, thank you. Somehow I feel the need to move around. Can you explain that feeling?" replied the President. "Now, what's this all about, Admiral, General?" he asked in a tone showing some anger.

"Sir, we haven't been completely honest with you in the past," said General North, as the President stood in silence. "Events happened in '68 which somehow spiralled out of our control."

"Explain yourself, General!"

"When Congress passed the Homosexual Bill in that year, the American way of life was under threat!"

"Go on!" replied the President.

"J. Edgar, at the time a close friend and colleague, rang one morning asking me to visit The Hoover Institute of Technology, which in those days was used as a research centre by the FBI and the CIA and if possible bring Admiral Rasmussen."

"Why the Admiral?" asked the President.

"Hoover knew Rasmussen hated the homosexual acts taking place at sea amongst his crew."

"How does this involve the White House?" asked the President with annoyance.

"Sir, I'm getting to that. J. Edgar showed us early results of a new genetically engineered virus they were experimenting with, a virus only affecting the homosexual, which would be freely transmitted by their sexual acts," said the General.

"So you took it upon yourselves to play God!"

"No, Mr. President, it wasn't like that! The homosexual sector started to take control, displaying acts once only ever committed behind closed doors, but now manifested publicly. That's when we decided to join the cause."

"Did Nixon know?"

"Yes sir! And every president since Nixon, except yourself!"

"Then why wasn't I informed?"

"We saw no reason. Those involved were old, as most were dead and we thought it best to keep the secret and to let it die with us."

"Then these people accidentally stumbled onto the truth?" replied the President.

"Yes! Very inconvenient!" said the General.

"What are your intentions, gentlemen now that the truth has come out?"

"Kill them!" replied the Admiral, banging his fist heavily onto the table.

"That's illegal. I hope you have other options!" said the President, his tone icy with anger.

"Mr. President, they're too dangerous. One wrong word could damage America severely!" replied the Admiral.

"There must be some other way. I can't and won't condone wholesale slaughter of innocent people! Especially with what you two bastards have done," replied the president, banging his fist heavily on the desk top.

"What do you think would happen to this office if the press got word?" replied the General. "Watergate would seem like a kindergarten picnic!"

"Sir, we have the perfect solution and opportunity," said the Admiral. "Their plane could disappear from radar on the return flight. All our problems would be solved!"

"Your problems not mine. And what about the crew aboard the aircraft?"

"What about them? They'd have sacrificed all for their country."

"You're not serious General! Your antics in playing God have already cost more lives lost than happened in all the world wars and minor skirmishes throughout history. You lot created AIDS, you bastards."

"We didn't create anything. But we agree with what happened," said the General.

"This meeting is over," the President said in a firm voice, emphasizing his anger at the conversation that had taken place.

The tape ended with a tiny click.

"Allan, did you know about this?" asked Clint.

"No, I didn't. I'm as shocked as you."

"Then what can we do about it?" asked Mick.

"Play it by ear, see what he has to offer. There's not really a great deal you can do," replied Allan. The problem is the selected people still active in the cover-up are only on file in the White House computer, with all access blocked."

"That's not a problem," replied Mick, smiling reassuringly at Linda.

"Please don't! You'll only get caught. Allow my people to do some searching. Hopefully I still have friends in the right places."

"I quite agree. Let Allan handle things. Let's just get away from here alive," said Linda.

"They wouldn't dare," said Peta, her arm firmly around Dusty's waist.

"Please, ladies, don't test them. We don't know who else could be involved" replied Allan, quietly excusing himself then departing the room.

"I think it's a good idea that we all stay together tonight," said Linda.

"Most certainly," replied Mick, as Dusty and Peta disappeared to the balcony.

"Nathan, let's see what the girls are up to," said Mick, heading for the doors.

The day slipped slowly into night and nothing further was said about the earlier events that partially crushed their total belief in the White House but not the American president. The meal served in the privacy of their room at the request of Clint had been exquisite and had everyone settled calmly for the night. Mick and Nathan had convinced the Southern girls, as if they needed convincing, to stay the night. The two girls had no commitments to anyone as they were both single as were the boys. With youth at their beckoning call, fun became the number one priority.

Chapter 33

Clint woke early to the sound of the doors creaking gently shut as the young ladies quietly departed, returning to the outside room before being missed by the oncoming Marines patrolling the halls.

"General, I don't like what's going on," crackled over the speaker, left on from the previous night.

"Admiral, I can't see a way out. We can't afford another killing. Not like Kennedy," came from the speaker. Clint moved closer to the speaker, the name Kennedy ringing loudly in his ears.

"Why not?" asked one voice.

"Are you serious? This time there's no Hoover to cover our ass!"

"We can't let these people walk!" said the same voice.

"I don't see that we have a choice!"

"There's always a choice," came the cynical reply. "I think we'd better stop! I'm sure these walls have ears, and the portraits tongues. You know how this office leaks."

"What about the President? How are we going to deal with him?"

"Admiral Samuel, nothing will happen. They can't afford the truth. Believe me!"

The doors slammed shut, and the speaker returned to silence. Clint remained quiet, his mind flashing back to that ill-fated day in November all those years ago. He knew now who the second party at the shooting was and in his own good time would make amends.

* * *

The morning passed quickly and now it was time to continue their meeting with the President started the previous day and somehow convince him that the secret of the virus was safe with them. Then they needed to negotiate a deal to benefit the suffering and the long dead killed by the HIV virus.

"Good morning. Come in," said the President standing by the doors with Linda the first to enter.

"Where is everyone?" she queried cautiously, for only Allan, General North and Admiral Rasmussen were present, standing and waiting.

"Linda I would prefer to keep the matter in house. However I would like you to meet General North and Admiral Rasmussen," replied the President, but he wasn't the same sure, confident person they had spoken to earlier. Today he seemed conservative and apprehensive, hesitantly unsure of himself as though asking questions from within.

"Any decision about our problem?" he asked, looking at the General and the Admiral.

"Yes, Mr. President. But understand this. Before we continue, copies of the film and manuscript will be released to the homosexual sector in San Francisco if any harm comes to any of us," replied Mick, smiling coldly at the Admiral, who looked to the General with surprise.

"Don't tell me you don't trust your President?" said the Admiral.

"Yes sir, we do! But if you gentlemen would care to listen to a tape I recorded yesterday, you may even recognize the voices, then perhaps you will understand my caution," said Mick, a half smile retained as he placed the recorder on the table and then pressed play. "I've already phoned the message out, so this is no longer the only copy!"

"Gentlemen, this is getting us nowhere," said the President, showing astonishment and embarrassment that Mick had a tape of their earlier conversation.

"Mr. President, these people bugged the Oval Office! That's treason!" yelled the Admiral, trying desperately to remove the attention from the tape.

"Samuel, will you please be quiet!" the President replied angrily. "Sorry, please continue." The silence in the room became intense as Bill replied.

"Out of no choice we agree to keep silent and that's against all our strongest beliefs, but conditions will most definitely apply," said Bill.

"And what obnoxious conditions might they be?" asked the Admiral, showing no signs of remorse.

"This office will release a complete list of names of the people missing from The Hoover Institute during the experimental stage of the virus, the people you helped murder," said Bill, trying purposely to stir up the Admiral.

"Mr. President!" the Admiral shouted. "I don't have to sit and take their crap. I had nothing to do with the so-called murders."

"Perhaps. But you could have prevented the slaughter," said Mick, his voice becoming louder with the General arguing in the background.

"Don't you people realize how many of us are sick to death of the homosexual minority flaunting their wares in public?" said the Admiral.

"No! You tell us," Linda replied, with disgust heavy in her tone. "Those people have rights. They're not out there killing with a passion like you two, they're living a reality. I'm sure it's not their choice to be gay. Life's played a cruel trick with their genes."

"Really!" shouted Rasmussen. "Do you realize that in Down Under and best forgotten Australia, there's a gay and lesbian Mardi-Gras held every year? They're taking over! Last year, fifty thousand people paraded their assorted wares through the streets of Sydney and a further million watched. Don't you think that's sick?"

"This is getting us nowhere," interrupted the President. "Would you gentlemen please excuse yourselves?" he said, gesturing with his hand to the door.

Bill caught the glare of defiance in their eyes, standing silently and staring at the faces around the room.

"This is not how it ends," said General North, letting the heavy doors close firmly behind him.

"You can be sure of that!" yelled Clint loudly trying to reach their ears through the closed doors. He turned to the President

"What do you think was meant by that last remark?" asked Clint of the President, knowing full well that someday soon he would hopefully have his confrontation.

"The General is an ambiguous bastard, but not game to cross me. I can keep those two in hand."

"Those two frighten me," said Linda, her voice fading softly as she held Bill's hand tightly.

"I'm truly sorry for their presence and I wish to apologize for their outbursts. Now, what's the second part of your request?" the President said calmly.

"Have everyone at the White House involved in the cover-up resign immediately, except yourself, Mr. President!"

"I see! But what would that prove?"

"Honesty back in the White House," replied Bill. "A Presidency where race colour or sexual preferences are no longer discriminated against."

"Bill, I don't condone homosexuality!"

"Sir, I can understand that, personally I feel the same, but these people need protection!" answered Bill.

"We have a long way to go and a long day ahead," replied the President.

"Allan, have you anything to add?" asked Linda.

"No. I think you've covered everything."

"Then let's move on," said Linda, standing and stretching her legs, Peta doing likewise.

* * *

Talking quietly and fruitfully for hours behind the massive hand carved doors, they slowly came to terms with the funding needed to help the stricken and educate against the ignorance and prejudice shown against the AIDS sufferer.

"Mick?" asked the president politely. "Before leaving my office would you mind removing your microphone?"

"Mr. President, that won't be necessary! The bug self-destructed after eighteen hours. I'm sorry, but I had to know!"

The president acknowledged by smiling and nodding approval.

The military jet was due to depart early afternoon, returning them to San Francisco. With the meeting over and each party satisfied with the outcome, they returned to the comfort of their quarters, the bags stored neatly by the door awaiting the journey home.

* * *

They landed early morning with the spotlights from the Air Force gunship lighting up the lawn. Both dogs were quick to respond, but became frightened by the noise of the thumping of the blades.

On departing the helicopter, the lieutenant in charge saluted Clint farewell, and then the deafening noise of the blades started as the aircraft disappeared into the darkness of night.

Two days had gone by since returning home from Washington. On the third, Howard and Hamish rang.

"Sorry, Howard," said Bill. "I should have phoned you when we first returned, but I needed to be sure if he would keep his word."

"Are you referring to the President, Bill? What's really going on?" asked Howard.

"Nothing that I'm aware of!" replied Bill.

"But the sackings, don't they mean anything?" asked Howard.

"What sackings?" asked Bill watching the girls entering the pool.

"All the names released to the early press. Do we know which people were involved in the conspiracy?" continued Howard, now anxious to get to the bottom of things

"Yes! Absolutely," replied Bill

"Then what are their names?" inquired Howard.

"Howard, I still don't trust the phone. Can we meet later to discuss the entire issue?" said Bill.

"I get your point. You better turn on the world news, he's making a public announcement some time today!" replied Howard.

"Howard, I feel we were being persuaded! He's honest beyond question, but I think he is under enormous pressure from within."

"From who?" asked Howard.

"His Chiefs of Staff!" replied Bill.

"Are they also involved?" said Howard.

"Some are. Some aren't!" answered Bill. "The two that are, are desperate and plain fucking dangerous!"

"Let's get off the phone. I'll get Hamish, and we'll be over directly. Have some names ready. By the way, Linda has another letter again hand delivered," replied Howard, hanging up the phone.

* * *

Howard and Hamish arrived within the hour and they lunched together on the balcony, continuing where they had left off earlier on the phone with the TV in the background playing old reruns of westerns best forgotten.

"So far, nine high-ranking officials have resigned or been sacked. Don't you find that fascinating? I'd love to know what's going on. Even do an article about the sackings!" said Howard.

"Howard, this is one we'll leave alone!" replied Clint. "Allow me in time to deal with them in my own way."

"Bill, I asked you the question earlier. What's really happening?" asked Howard with Hamish smiling quietly in the background.

Bill went to reply but was interrupted by Linda returning with another bottle of bubbly firmly in hand.

"Watch the television - the President is about to make a public announcement!" she said moving in close to Bill wrapping her arm tightly around his torso

"Ladies and gentlemen, the President of the United States," came the squawking voice of the commentator.

"My fellow Americans. There has been widespread speculation by the press in the past few days about the sackings of some high-ranking officials in Washington. The FBI and the CIA have uncovered a plot by certain people in our armed forces to mislead the American people. These few have now been dealt with and there will be no further witch-hunt or bloodletting. Details will not be released at this point in time, for it would greatly undermine this wonderful nation of ours.

"Furthermore, unrelated to the announcement, I wish to announce a fifteen billion dollar on-going program to help with the fight against AIDS. No longer can we sit back and hope the issue goes away. We all know that the cocktail of drugs now available in this great country of ours works in the fight against AIDS. We can't cure the virus, but we can prolong the quality and quantity of life of those infected. These programs are very expensive to administer throughout the developing countries, but I feel compelled to do something to help these nations in their hour of need. Legislation is at this very moment passing through the

Senate preventing the prejudices that exist towards the HIV-positive person. And to also to help us better understand their plight.

"God bless America."

The broadcast ended as it had begun, suddenly.

"Well, he did as he said," said Mick, the sun now piercing through the pergola.

"Now all we need is a list of those who perished in the experimental stage," replied Linda, the girls with Nathan moving back to the pool.

"Well, Bill, you got your story," said Dusty, again locked in a friendly game of chess with Clint.

"But I can't use it!" replied Bill.

"Can't you write about the compassionate conclusion?" asked Dusty with Peta still by his side hanging on tight to his left arm.

"Dusty, it wouldn't make sense! There isn't one."

"Then what are you going to write about?" asked Clint, looking closely at Bill.

"I'm not sure! Perhaps a story about the sick society we're creating!" replied Bill smiling.

"I don't follow!" replied Dusty, Bill now having their undivided attention.

"The colour barrier and the assaults on each other's person, rape, murder, deceit, mistrust, you name it. We do it. Also the people guarded with our trust, the people in charge. The politicians lining their pockets to further their own needs!" said Bill then snapping back to reality.

"What's the answer?" asked Clint, his eyes now returned to the board.

"I don't have an answer, or pretend to know one!" Bill replied, pausing, looking closely at the latest moves performed by Clint and Dusty trying desperately to find each other's weakness at the game. "Sorry, I think I'm getting carried away,"

"Don't apologize! I think we all feel the same," replied Mick, standing to join the girls at the pool.

"Another letter addressed to Linda arrived this morning!" said Howard sipping from his ice cold beer presented earlier by Peta.

"Read it, dad!" was Linda's reply.

Howard reached into his back pocket and brought out the letter. He unfolded it and began reading.

"Friends," the letter began. *"You have done well. You have punished those responsible in the White House. The White House is finally cleansed for the first time in forty years. Jack would be proud of you all. Prodi and Ramos are still out there but I suppose that Father Time will slowly take his toll upon the duo. I have tried in vain to locate their whereabouts but they are as elusive as the night. I hope that in the near future we will be destined to meet for I would be honoured just to shake your hands. God bless you all. A friend!*

Chapter 34

The weeks passed, and there was not a day when there wasn't something in the media about AIDS. The latest movie was about the Ebola outbreak in Africa, with Dustin Hoffman playing the heroic doctor who isolated an entire village, saving the world from this killer virus. It sounded almost as though someone had read from the Carlos pages about Zaire and the sudden death of the entire village. But that wouldn't be possible, for only they and the President knew the real story. Perhaps the movie came from the documentation recorded in the early seventies. Nobody would ever know the real story about the Zaire massacre except that it really happened. And sadly, nobody cared.

A few days later, faxed through to Howard's office came the complete list of those murdered at the Hoover institute. Half way down the list the name Stuart Wallace appeared - younger brother to Hamish. The names read like a Who's Who of the missing persons of that era. Out of respect Howard, with Hamish's help, released a special obituary edition, the all but forgotten names released to an unknowing public.

Dusty, together with Peta, returned to Haiti for a brief visit to renew their friendship with young Pedro, then later retrieved Carlos' remains from Columbia - if he had indeed died there.

The key with the microfilm belonged to a safety deposit box, the back of the clipping showed a Navaho Indian standing beside the San Francisco International Merchant Bank. Inside the safety deposit box was a small diary containing the names of Carlos and Peta in joint accounts, with a note assuring her the money - and there were several millions - was not drug-related. The diary also contained the ancient alphabet and hieroglyphics of the forgotten Navaho. The ancient wording and drawing's would help decipher the code of the Anasazi Indian should the need arise. Attached for the world to read were the words of the human beings.

"Treat the earth and all that dwell thereon with respect."

Nathan and Saara returned home to Nevada and with promised help from Allan and the President, supervised the building of a modern AIDS clinic to help the American Indians and the fight against HIV and associated prejudices.

Clint briefly returned to Washington DC to the grave of his beloved President. He still bore the guilt for the slaying of John Fitzgerald Kennedy.

"All these years I protected these people! The watchdogs that ordered you slain!" he said quietly under his breath. Then the anger got to him. "I should have known!" he yelled, the words echoing loudly throughout Arlington.

He stood for hours in silence, neither eye nor muscle stirring, staring deeply at the eternal flame hoping for a sign, the mark of forgiveness.

He returned to the grave every day for a week then joined the siblings in Nevada to help with the fight against the virus. He would later seek out North and Rasmussen and in his own time, administer the justice that was long overdue them.

Together with Nathan and Saara they placed a marble headstone over 73's ashes, the inscription reading simple, *"Here rests Antonio Demagos. He trusted the wrong people in life, but gave his all in death. God have pity on his soul."* On the back of the headstone, a smaller inscription: *"Thank you for your help! You will be avenged. The world will one day know you were a true legend."*

Linda and Howard resurrected the Weekly and with Hamish's help quickly regained a strong following.

Bill went quietly back to work finishing his story on AIDS. He called the article *'Philadelphia'*. Perhaps one day someone would make a film depicting the plight of and bias towards the HIV sufferer. He desperately wanted to write the complete story and name names but knew that discretion was the better part of valour. He kept all his notes in his private diary and deep down hoped that someday perhaps after his death someone would read and tell the truth about this man-made holocaust and the people responsible.

Chapter 35

Two weeks had passed, as Bill sitting in his office was hard at work when Mick stepped through the door.

"You rang, my Lord?" he said sarcastically.

"Mick, do you still have copies of the manuscript, the microfilm and the Washington tape?" asked Bill leaning back in his chair with his hands behind his head.

"No! I never did," Mick replied, taken by surprise. "That was all a bluff to get out of there alive."

"Shit, I was really hoping!" said Bill.

"Hoping what?" asked Mick as Linda entered the office, her perfume wafting sweetly in the air.

"Sorry to interrupt you two," she said, staring directly at last year's nude calendar still holding centre stage. "Here are the files you requested earlier."

Mick looked over her shoulder, trying to read the papers. "What are you working on now?" he asked, feeling he could be of some service.

"I'm completing the story we started, but now I can add the dark side!" said Bill.

"Dark side?" queried Linda.

"Yes, the people involved from the beginning. Names, dates, place, everything makes sense now!" replied Bill.

"But we promised the President," she quietly replied.

"And our promise will be honoured. The story will never go to print."

"Then why do it?" asked Mick, as confused as Linda.

"Protection. They wouldn't dare try anything if they knew we had the complete story!"

"Are you still worried about Ramos and Prodi?" asked Mick.

"No, I'm more worried about the other two clowns, North and Rasmussen," replied Bill.

"It's been weeks. If anything was going to happen, it would have happened by now," replied Mick.

"Perhaps I'm paranoid!" said Bill. "But I really feel this is something I have to do. If not for myself, then for those murdered by the system and ridiculed for it!"

"I can live with that," replied Mick as Shelly joined them.

"What are we discussing?" she asked, placing a tray of coffee on the table.

"Old times," replied Linda.

"Times best left alone," Shelley said.

"Nothing is best left alone! If you don't use it! You lose it!" replied Shelly smiling then winking one eye at Mick and he winking back.

Chapter 36

A week passed, and then a small clipping from the New York Centennial appeared on Bill's desk. The caption read simply:

Victoria Prodi and Victor Ramos, both former FBI agents, have been found dead in what police describe as suspicious circumstances. Miss Prodi was discovered deceased in her hotel room in New York, with no tell-tale marks to her body. There was however a small necklace dating back to the ancient Anasazi Indians around her neck. Mr. Ramos, her close associate over the years was discovered in his apartment in California, dead, also without clues. He too wore the identical necklace. However, the baffling part of the mystery is that their watches both stopped at precisely the same moment. The investigating police are completely mystified and baffled by the circumstances surrounding their deaths.

The old Indian had somehow taken revenge then returned home to his beloved Valley of Ten Thousand Smokes. He had said that the outer spirit of the body can travel the expanse of time in the blink of an eye...

Bill immediately rang Nathan and Saara in Nevada to confirm the deaths and to ask how the charms found around their necks had played a significant part in their demise, also, to ask Nathan's grandfather for permission to run the story of the Human Beings. Nathan informed Bill that since returning home he had discovered that his grandfather, the old Indian had passed away years earlier.

* * *

Mick became background researcher to the magazine, assuring Howard he wouldn't use the decoder even in the most extreme emergency. Shelly and he had become a pair, her innocence blended with his brilliance. Her sexuality cancelled out his shyness and her openness negated his seclusion.

It was late Friday afternoon when Mick entered Howard's office.

"Look," he said, holding some papers over his head.

"What's this?" replied Howard with surprise.

"This article," said Mick, placing the papers on Howard's desk. "Cancer research."

"Cancer research?" asked Howard.

"Yes, about how it was suspended in the late thirties. Suspended by the Great American Scalpel," replied Mick with a broad smile on his face.

"And what exactly is the Great American Scalpel?"

"The surgeons of America. They were making shitloads of money cutting out rather than curing cancer. Then, in the fifties, when sanity finally prevailed and research resumed, the drug companies took control. Not to find a cure but simply to keep the patient alive, hopefully for up to five years."

"Why five years?" inquired Howard, thinking he'd missed something in their conversation.

"That's how long it takes the average American family to deplete their medical insurance," replied Mick.

"Are you telling me the drug companies don't want to cure cancer?" asked Howard.

"Absolutely! When the insurance runs out, so do they! The drug companies don't give a rat's ass about curing cancer. They only see the mighty dollar and what makes it worse, our politicians are in bed with them!" replied Mick with his voice rising to anger.

"Where the fuck did you get your information?" asked Howard, but looking at Shelly, short skirt blended with a see-through blouse and standing proudly beside Mick.

"Howard, it's now late Friday afternoon and we can be in and out of Level Four before we're noticed. Could be an awesome story and one that needs telling," said Mick, with a sheepish look on his face.

"What the hell is Level Four?" asked Howard.

"Central Medical is the main computer. And nothing's been erased – yet!" replied Mick now smiling broadly with one arm around Shelly

Howard looked at both, slowly shaking his head.

"Howard! God Bless America," said Mick as he and Shelly departed the office.

Definitely, not the end.

www.ingramcontent.com/pod-product-compliance
Lightning Source LLC
Chambersburg PA
CBHW072231170626
46813CB00003B/1173